The Boy
Who Fell
From the Sky

Dan Bomkamp

Lovstad Publishing
www.Lovstadpublishing.com

Printed in the United States of America

THE BOY WHO FELL FROM THE SKY

ISBN: 0692490973
ISBN-13: 978-0692490976
Previous ISBN: 0692467106

Cover design by Lovstad Publishing

For Mom and Dad

Acknowledgments

Thanks to Skyler Ewers and Maggie
for portraying Anton and Patrick on the cover.

Thanks as usual to my publisher and friend
Joel Lovstad for his work putting the books together.

The Boy
Who Fell
From the Sky

Chapter 1

It was hot. It had been a terribly hot day and now in the evening, it was still nearly eighty degrees. The air felt like it was coming from an oven. It was stifling in the tent. In addition to being hot it was also terribly humid. The air felt so wet Anton Sands could hardly breathe. It reminded him of once when he had been at a friend's house and they'd gone into their sauna. It was like trying to breathe under water. He was lying on his sleeping bag with sweat running off his body. He tossed and turned.

"I can't sleep like this," he said more to himself than anyone. His dog, Patrick lifted his head and began panting.

"It's too hot Patrick. Let's go outside."

At the sound of the word 'outside' Patrick jumped up and stood by the tent door wagging his tail. He opened the door and Patrick bounded through into the humid night.

He laid his sleeping bag out onto the grass and slipped his tee shirt and shorts on. He lay on top of the sleeping bag. Once it was dark the mosquitoes usually weren't a problem but even if there were some, it was better than cooking inside the tent. It was a heck of a lot better than being in the house down the valley.

"I bet our bedroom at the house is ninety degrees," he said.

The house was indeed hot in the summer. It was a typical farmhouse in that it was a big box with a kitchen, dining room and living room on the ground floor and four bedrooms on the second floor. It was clad in white siding and had a black roof and was typical of thousands of farm houses standing on a long flowing lawn out in the middle of nowhere. His parents had a window air-conditioner in their room and offered to have Anton and Patrick sleep in there on the hot nights but he was a teenager and didn't think it was right for him to sleep with his folks.

The one thing that made it better was that the house had a wrap-around porch that went across the front and down both sides of it. There was some wicker furniture with pads on it on the porch, and one piece was a couch. He and Patrick had slept on the couch many times when it was hot in the upstairs bedroom. This night would have been a bad one in the house but the tent on the creek bank was much better. He thought back to the first day he'd seen his new home. It was a big change from what he was used to.

The barn had burned down years before. There was a garage and a building that once had been a chicken house that was now a storage shed. Below the house about a hundred yards away a small creek ran through the fields. The house had been built in the 1920's and it looked every bit of the 90 years it had stood on that spot

Anton and his parents had only lived there for a few months. His dad Brad got a job, teaching math at the college one town down the road and his mom Sandy got a job at the hospital in town as a nurse.

They'd lived in Ohio before coming to Wisconsin and this country living was just what his parents had been looking for. Anton was used to kids all up and down the street and being able to get on a bus and go to the movies or to the mall whenever he wanted. The closest he came to other kids was when they went to town. He hoped to meet some new friends in the fall when he started school but for now, he was on his own. This was as far away from civilization as he'd ever been. Normally he would be with friends from the sub-division all day long. Now it was he and Patrick.

Before they moved he spent his days playing X-Box or other video games with his friends or taking a bus to the mall and running around the mall for the day. Here he was alone in the outdoors and the closest thing to a mall was Walmart.

He was beginning to get used to it and the fact that his parents had allowed him to get a dog really sealed the deal. He'd pestered them for weeks about a dog and they'd finally given in. They'd gone to a shelter to find a dog that needed a home and the minute he saw the beagle sitting in a cage staring at him he knew that was his dog.

He looked at Patrick lying on his back sleeping and he thought back to that day at the animal shelter. He and his mom had walked along the rows of cages, looking at the dogs that needed homes. There were some mixed breeds, and some hunting dogs like Labradors. There were two little terriers that barked constantly while they looked at them. Then he'd seen the beagle. He'd gotten on his knees in front of the cage. The dog had looked at him but not showed any interest in getting closer.

"How are you?" he'd said.

The dog's tail swished on the cement floor.

"Can you come here?

The dog got up and walked over to him. He stuck his fingers in the cage and the dog looked at them.

"Come here boy," he said.

The dog stepped closer and licked his fingers.

"Good boy. What's your name?"

"He doesn't speak English," his mom said grinning.

Anton looked up and felt foolish.

"Sorry I was just making conversation with him."

"He's a dog honey. Do you like him?"

Anton nodded. "He's perfect," he said.

He looked at the dog. He had sad brown eyes and his long

ears made him look even sadder. But he had a sparkle in those eyes that told Anton he had a lot of fun left in him.

The shelter person told them that the dog had belonged to an older lady who had passed away. He was used to living in the house and a very friendly dog. She said he seemed very sad after losing his human.

"Does he have a name?" Anton asked.

"His name is Patrick," the lady said.

"Patrick. That's a strange name for a dog," he said.

The lady laughed. "Her former husband who died some years ago was also named Patrick. I guess she liked that name. You can call him anything you like and he'd adjust to it."

"I like Patrick," Anton said.

"Do you want this one or do you want to keep looking?" his mom asked.

"I want him."

So they opened the cage and Patrick walked out and sat down in front of Anton. He looked up into his face and raised his right paw.

"Oh gosh, he wants to shake hands," Anton said.

He took the dog's paw and they shook. Then the dog got up and stood looking at him.

"I think he likes you," the shelter lady said.

"We'll take him."

Patrick walked by his side to the office and stood there wagging his tail as they paid for him and got all of his papers. Anton couldn't keep the smile off his face.

Chapter 2

Anton and Patrick became best friends over the next few weeks. Although Anton was only thirteen his dad felt that he was responsible enough to have a 4-wheeler so they bought a used one and strapped a plastic milk crate on the back of it. After a few tries, Patrick figured out he had to sit still in the crate and he and his master could fly over the trails on the farm and have wonderful times. They'd ride up and down the valley and the dog's ears would flap in the wind. He loved riding with his new master.

There was a creek down in the valley that looked like a great place to spend some time. Anton rode his bike along the creek far up into the valley. It varied in width and depth but he saw fish flash away quite often as he rode along. Patrick watched the water as if he was looking for fish too.

They came to a low area where the land turned wet and muddy. He parked his bike and walked toward the marshy looking area.

"Let's go look," he said to the dog.

Patrick took off sniffing the puddles and clumps of grass while Anton took off his shoes and socks. He walked through the wet ground that soon turned to mud. There were clumps of willows and cattails and small puddles of water here and there.

As they got farther up into the marsh, a duck flew up from ahead of them. Patrick took off chasing it but soon came back.

There were frogs and it looked like a muskrat house farther

into the wetland.

"This is a cool place," he said to the dog.

Patrick wagged his tail. They walked through the mud and eventually the ground began to firm up. The marsh turned back into a small creek and it went up into the next valley.

"I bet the spring that feeds this creek is up there," he said.

They turned around and went back to where his four-wheeler was parked. He waded into the creek and washed his feet off. Patrick was all covered with mud so Anton washed him off too. Then they rode down the bank toward the house.

Anton took a look at the creek on his way back and found a couple of places that looked like they might be a place to catch a fish. He loved fishing so he got his pole and dug some worms and soon he and Patrick were sitting on the bank waiting for a bite. The stream was only about eight feet across and not very deep, so the fishing wasn't very good. He caught a few suckers now and then but not much else. Patrick was content to lay in the grass and let Anton stroke his silky ears. He got very excited when his master caught the first fish. They fished for an hour without much happening. Anton decided to try a new spot.

They walked up the creek for a long way and found a spot where it was very narrow. Above that spot the creek was twice as wide as the lower part. It was like a pool.

They sat on the bank of the wide spot and Anton caught three suckers and then caught a nice trout. This was the best spot. He decided that he'd fish here from now on. He looked at the wide hole and at the narrow shallow riffles below it. He suddenly had a great idea.

"We could make this into a pond," he told the dog.

Patrick wagged his tail.

"This is a good spot. We need some rocks, and then we can build a dam and make the hole deeper and wider."

They went back to the house and got the 4-wheeler and drove along the hills that bordered the valley. They checked out many rocky areas but didn't find the right kind of stones for building a dam. Most were big boulders that he couldn't move and the rest were little stones that would just be washed away. They drove farther and were just above the pond site when Anton found a place where the hillside had caved away. There was a pile of dirt, sod and rocks at the bottom of the hill. It was just what he was looking for.

"I need a rack for the 4-wheeler," he told his parents that evening at dinner.

"What for Honey?" his mom asked.

"I'm going to dam up the stream and make a pond. Patrick and I can fish there and take a swim and it will be a nice place to camp."

His dad grinned.

"It's going to take a lot of work."

"I've got all summer," he said.

So the next day his dad stopped at the dealer where they'd bought the vehicle and bought a steel rack that bolted to the back of the frame. They used bungee cords to attach Patrick's crate to the rack and it still left a lot of room for stones for the dam.

Anton could hardly wait for the next day to start construction on his dam.

"We need some big ones for the bottom," he said to Patrick as he dragged a large stone toward the vehicle.

He got the stone to the vehicle but it was much too heavy for him to lift up onto the rack. He stood there scratching his head.

"How are we gonna get this up there?" he asked the dog.

Patrick walked over to the rock, sniffed it and then peed on it.

Anton laughed.

"That's not gonna help Patrick," he said scratching the dog's ears.

"We need a plank and a come-along."

They went to the garage and he found just what he was looking for. The previous owners had left some stuff behind and one of the things was a contraption that they used to pull fence wires tight when they built a fence. He figured he could attach it to the vehicle and then tie the other end around the rock and work it up onto the vehicle with the come-along if he could find a plank to slide it on.

There was an old manure spreader in the middle of a big weed patch out back where the barn used to be and he found a 2 x 12 plank in a pile of old lumber.

"This is just what we need."

He and Patrick drove back up to the rockslide and he backed up by the rock. He wedged the plank under the edge of the rack and tied the come-along to the seat bracket. Then he tied the rope on the other end to the rock and began working the lever back and forth. It took a few cranks to get the rope tight but then each time he pulled the lever the rock moved a few inches.

He had it half way up the plank when he noticed it was getting off center so he stopped and pushed it back to the middle of the plank. Then he cranked it all the way up to the rack. He slid it onto the rack and untied the rope.

"Nothing to it Patrick. Now all we need is about a hundred more rocks."

Over the next few weeks they made many trips from the hill to the creek. He quickly found that he couldn't overload the four-wheeler. The second time he loaded it up he put too many rocks on it and when he started driving toward the creek, the front wheels came off the ground and he couldn't steer. So he had to stop and take some rocks off. He decided from then on to make lighter loads and more trips. Each time they hauled rocks, when they got to the creek Anton rolled the rocks off the rack and down over the creek bank to the ever-growing pile of rocks in the narrow part of the stream. Then he'd take off his shoes and socks and wade into the creek and lift the new rock up on top of the ever-growing dam. Each time the dam grew a few inches higher and wider.

By the 4th of July he had all the rocks he needed. The dam was three feet high and about six feet wide. The trouble was that the pile of rocks was pretty unstable. He quickly found out that he'd built it too narrow when the whole thing fell over into the lower part of the creek. He was pretty frustrated but he re-built the dam and made it wider at the bottom so it was more stable. When he finished it the second time, there was a lot of water running through the rocks yet but the pond had grown a lot and the dam was solid.

"We need some of that sod up there to fill the holes," he said.

He remembered seeing a beaver dam and how the beavers had packed sod and weeds into the holes in the dam to seal it. There were big chunks of sod on the hill where the ground had slipped away when the rocks slid down so he had some packing material.

He and Patrick hauled chunks of sod from the hill to the pond. When he had a big pile of sod pieces he took off his shoes and shirt and waded into the water on the upstream side of the dam. He carried a chunk of sod with him and shoved it into a hole between rocks to plug the hole. One by one he filled the holes with sod. Each time he packed a hole full, less water leaked from the pond.

Eventually the dam was pretty solid and even though there were some small leaks it held water back as he had hoped.

While the dam was holding water back it looked like it might topple if too much pressure was put on it if the water got higher in a rain storm. He didn't want to do all this work and then have it tip over again. He pushed against it from below the dam and the thing wiggled. That definitely was not a good sign.

"We need some logs to shore it up," he told Patrick. The dog wagged.

He took the next days hauling logs and branches from the hill to the pond where he cut them to the right length with a hand saw and then wedged them between the creek banks against the sod and rocks. Then he wedged some heavy timbers below until his dam was as solid as if it had been there for years. It was wide enough on top for him and Patrick to walk across it.

He and the dog stood on top of the dam looking at their pond. The pond was about twenty feet wide and at least forty feet long before it went back to a narrow stream.

Below them the water gurgled over the top of the dam and a bit seeped through. There was enough water going over and through it that the creek was as if it hadn't been changed a bit.

"We did it Patrick."

The dog wagged. He looked up at his master with adoring eyes.

"Let's take a swim."

He walked to the bank and took off his clothes. Then he carefully crept down over he bank to the edge of the water. Patrick followed him.

"Well here goes," he said.

He jumped into the water. It was cold but not so cold that he couldn't stand it.

"Come on in Patrick," he coaxed the dog.

Patrick stood there for a minute and then took a mighty leap and landed in the pond. He came paddling to his master. They swam and Anton laughed and laughed as they played in the water.

After half an hour he climbed out and wiped the water from his body. He put his clothes on and they drove back to the house.

"You have to see my pond," he said that night at dinner.

"How's it coming?" his dad asked.

"It's done."

"Really?"

"Can you guys come up and see it?"

"Of course, right after dinner," his dad said.

They drove his dad's jeep up to the pond. His parents were open-mouthed when they saw the pond.

"Oh my goodness, I had no idea it was this big," his dad said, staring at the pond.

"You did this all by yourself?" his mom asked.

"Me and Patrick."

His parents were impressed to say the least. His dad looked at the dam and said it was very well constructed. His mom worried that the water was too deep and he might drown.

"Mom I can swim like a fish," he said.

"But that was in a pool, this is... well it's different."

His dad came to his defense.

"You know what would be the finishing touch?" his dad asked.

"What?"

"I'll call one of he local contractors and have them bring a load of sand up here. You show them where you want your beach and they can dump the sand on the bank and into the edge of the pond so you'll have a nice sandy beach to go in and out of instead of all of these weeds."

"Oh man that would be great," he said.

The next day Anton took the lawn mower up and mowed off a spot where the beach would be. The next day a big dump truck drove down their lane and the driver stopped at the house. Anton had the guy follow him up to the pond. They dumped the sand on the edge of the pond and Anton took a rake and smoothed it out.

So a few days later Anton had his own private lake and beach. Life was good.

Chapter 3

The sand had been dumped on a gradual sloping area of the creek bank and it made a beach that was about fifteen feet square. Anton hauled the lawn mower down to the pond on the 4-wheeler and cut the weeds down so the place was like a little park in the middle of the pasture.

He and Patrick spent a lot of time there over the next weeks. They'd take lunch down to the pond in the morning when his parents went to work and then they'd fish and usually would take a swim.

There was a huge maple tree on the other side of the pond and Anton noticed a big branch that stuck out over the water. It didn't take long for him to get an idea and a few hours later he'd climbed the tree and tied a rope from the branch. Then he pulled the rope back to the opposite bank and swung out on it and dropped into the pond. Patrick ran around barking crazily when Anton flew through the air.

One day his dad came home with a long box that turned out to be a tent. He and his dad took it to the pond and set it up. It was perfect.

"Can I sleep down here tonight?" he asked.

"If your mother is okay with it," his dad said smiling.

"This is really cool dad," Anton said hugging him.

"Are you okay out here all by yourself? Your mom and I worry that you're alone so much."

"I'm okay Dad, I have Patrick."

"Well, school will start in September and then you'll meet some kids and hopefully you'll be able to bring them home to share your pond with you."

"I bet a lot of kids will be impressed with my own private pond."

He slept in the tent with Patrick that night and for the next several weeks. Little by little he hauled stuff to the tent so it became his bedroom. He got an air mattress, a little wooden crate for clothes and stuff, a propane lantern, a radio and a cooler that he kept filled with snacks and sodas.

"We need a fire pit," he said one night as he and Patrick sat on the sand in front of the tent.

The next day they took the 4-wheeler up to the rockslide and he filled the rack with medium-sized rocks to build a fire pit. As he was picking rocks he noticed a triangle-shaped hole in the side of the hill, up several feet from the bottom. He climbed up as far as he could get and looked into the hole.

It was shaped like a triangle and looked like it was made of two slabs of rock that overlapped each other on either side. At the bottom there was just packed dirt but he could see inside and there was a hole that went back into the hillside for quite a long way.

"Maybe that's a cave," he told Patrick.

"We better check it out tomorrow. I'll get some tools."

He hauled his rocks back and built a fire pit. Then he and Patrick drove up into the woods and he loaded up the utility rack with branches for a fire. He unloaded them and went home for a hatchet and some digging tools.

He chopped the branches into fire-sized pieces and stacked them next to the tent. It was getting late so he and Patrick drove down to the house for dinner.

His parents acted like something was on their minds. His dad was grinning but his mom seemed uneasy.

"What's wrong?" Anton asked.

His mom looked at his dad and then nodded.

"Your mom and I have been talking about how responsible you are and I mentioned that when I was your age my dad bought me a trail bike."

Anton's eyes got wide.

"No way!"

"Look in the garage," his dad said, barely holding his excitement.

Anton ran to the garage and his parents followed. There sitting in the middle of the floor was a brand new Suzuki Off Road Trail Bike. It was bright yellow and the most beautiful thing Anton had ever seen.

"No way!"

His dad was very excited and he showed Anton all the features of the bike. His mom was less enthusiastic but she was happy to see her son so jubilant over the bike.

"Can I take it for a ride?"

"Do you know how to shift it and all of that?"

"Um no, but I bet you do," Anton said grinning at his dad.

Brad looked at his wife. She shook her head and grinned.

"I don't know which of you is the teenager. I'll go put dinner into the oven to keep it warm. You have fifteen minutes and then we'll eat. You can play afterward."

Anton and his dad rolled the bike out onto the driveway and his dad got on and showed him the shift pattern and the clutch and brake. Then he fired up the little bike and took off down the driveway. Anton watched him and knew his dad was reliving his childhood as much as teaching his son how to ride.

Brad came back and shut the bike off. He got off and grinned at his son.

"This thing has a ton of power. You have to promise to be careful with it. Take it easy until you figure out how it works."

Anton said he'd be real careful. He got on the bike and started it and then put it into first gear. He slowly gave it gas and let off on the clutch and soon he was going down the driveway slowly. Patrick was running alongside him barking. He got a little way down the road and shifted and gave the bike gas and he sped up a little. He had a grin as wide as could be as he turned and rode back toward the garage.

He got off the bike and wrapped his arms around his dad.

"You're the best dad in the world," he said. His dad smiled and a tear ran from his eye.

"Just please, please, don't crash it. Your mom will kill me if you get hurt on it."

"I'll be careful Dad, I promise."

They went in for dinner and Anton hugged his mom too.

"I know you had the final say on it," he said. "Thanks Mom, it's the coolest thing I've ever owned."

"You be careful on that thing. It's not a toy you know."

Anton looked at his dad and winked.

"I promise, I won't go very fast."

Chapter 4

Anton took the milk crate off the 4-wheeler and used bungee cords to fasten it to the back of his motorbike. He made sure it was secure and then he put Patrick in the crate.

"Okay, we'll go slow until you get used to this," he said as Patrick wagged his tail.

Anton fired up the bike and they took off up the valley. Patrick wagged his tail and seemed like he liked riding on the bike. Anton took that as a sign to go faster. He was getting the feel of the thing and he felt sure of himself, so he gave it more gas and off they went.

Riding the motorbike was a real thrill. At first Anton kept to the valley and rode out in the open but soon he followed a deer trail up into the edge of the woods and rode along it. That didn't last long because he came to a downed tree that had fallen across the trail. He stopped and looked at it and then he turned around.

He and Patrick drove down to the garage and got a limb saw and then went back up to the trail. When he got to the tree across the trail he parked the bike and got his saw and started cutting the tree. Patrick sniffed around and explored while he cleared the trail.

Once that tree was out of the way they started up again and followed the trail farther up the hill. He stopped now and then and cut branches and limbs off so he could ride the trail without getting smacked in the face with a branch. They came to the top of the hill where there was a field. There was a fence on the edge of the field.

"This must be the end of our land," he said to Patrick. He looked out across the field and then noticed that another trail ran along the fence. He turned and followed that trail and soon it went down into the woods. He followed it and cleared it and finally found himself in the valley farther up the hill from the house.

"We can figure out all of these trails and then we can go all over the place," he said to the dog. Patrick wagged his tail approvingly.

"Did you ride the Kawasaki today?" his dad asked when he got home.

"Yeah, we rode all day. Patrick likes riding on it," Anton said.

"I saw the crate. He's okay going fast?"

Anton saw the trap.

"We didn't go very fast Dad. We just explored."

His dad grinned.

"Yeah, I'll bet. Just be careful until you get used to it... and for God's sake don't crash it or your mother will kill me."

Anton grinned and nodded.

"I'll be careful. And Dad... thanks a million for it."

Over the next weeks Anton and Patrick found every trail on the farm. He cleared them and even cut a few new ones in areas there were none. He had a complete circuit of trails that he could ride and get to almost any part of the farm.

The only place he hadn't been was the next farm up the valley. He knew it was abandoned and that no one had lived there for a long time. So one day he and Patrick drove up to the end of the valley and found a trail that led up onto the farm.

"I don't think anyone would care if we rode up there," he said to the dog. "Besides, nobody lives there so no one will know."

They followed a trail that went up the hill at a pretty seep angle. It was harder going and there were a lot of branches to cut but after a couple of hours he was on the hillside above the old buildings.

He looked down and the place looked pretty bad. The house was all but falling down. The roof had holes in it and the front porch was nearly gone, having fallen in on itself. There was an old shed that looked fairly sturdy and a couple of small sheds that might have been for chickens.

"Not much left up here," he said.

There was a good-sized open field at the bottom of the valley that had been planted with crops in better times. He checked out the trail and it seemed to wind down to the valley floor so he followed it.

"The deer used to come down here and eat corn," he said.

He followed the trail and it went up the other side of the valley so he took that trail and cleared it out too. Then he found the highway up near the top.

"Wow, we've got miles of trails to ride Patrick." Patrick wagged his tail

Chapter 5

Patrick and Anton rode the trails and found all kinds of cool places to go on the farms. Once he got used to them he knew right where he was going and where he'd come out. Soon he got the idea to make some jumps to give the ride more excitement.

He took a shovel along and when he found a spot that looked good, he'd mound up the dirt on the trail and make a jump on it. The first time he jumped Patrick yelped, but soon he got so he liked the jumps too.

Later that day he and Patrick were flying down the valley toward home. He'd been riding for a long time and kind of forgotten the time. They were really moving when he flew up to the yard and there stood his mother.

"Oh boy," he said to himself.

"Anton, how fast were you going?"

"Not so fast Mom. This thing just looks like it's going fast because of the way it was designed."

"Baloney. I know fast when I see it. I thought you were going to be safe on that thing."

Just then his dad came out. He looked at Anton and shook his head quietly, telling him not to argue.

"Sandy, he's had the bike for a long time and hasn't put a scratch on it or himself. He's okay."

His mom shook her head.

"It's like dealing with two boys."

"That was unfortunate," his dad said after his mom went inside.

"I know. I didn't think you guys were home yet."

"So she goes pretty fast?"

Anton grinned. "Fast as the wind. I've got trails all over the woods and jumps and it's just so much fun."

His dad grinned.

"I wonder if she'd let me get one."

He and his dad laughed as they went into the house.

"Are you sleeping in the tent tonight?" his mom asked.

"I plan on it," he said.

"They're forecasting storms," his dad said.

"The tent's waterproof," he said.

"Yes it is but if it gets windy it might not hold up."

"Is it going to get windy?"

"There is a sixty percent chance of thunderstorms. They sometimes get pretty windy."

"If it gets bad I'll jump on the dirt bike and hurry home," he said.

That suited his parents. They ate dinner and then he and Patrick drove up the valley to the pond. He took off his shoes and socks and waded along the edge of the pond casting a little spinner out across the water. He'd caught three nice trout in the last few weeks so he thought some must have come down the creek and made their home in the bigger water at his pond.

He didn't get any strikes after fishing the length of the pond so he switched to a hook and sinker and a worm.

He and Patrick sat on the edge of the bank about half way up the pond. The dog sat right next to him watching him fish.

"You and I are pretty lucky Patrick. Not many kids my age have their own pond."

The dog wagged his tail.

After half an hour he got a bite and caught a big white

sucker. It gave him a good fight so he unhooked it and put it back to fight another day.

"Well, its getting dark," he said, "Time for a campfire."

They put the fishing gear away and he built a little pile of tiny branches in the middle of the fire pit. Then he wadded up some paper and lit it under the branches and soon he had a little fire going. He added some bigger branches and the fire took off. He and Patrick sat side-by-side and watched the flames dance, as it turned dark.

Patrick laid his head against Anton's leg and sighed. He looked down at the dog and petted his silky ears.

"You're a good boy," he said quietly.

Patrick's tail thumped on the sand.

They sat and watched the fire until it began to die down. Patrick raised his head and listened.

"What do you hear boy?"

They sat quietly and then Anton heard it too. There was thunder far off in the west. He watched and saw the sky brighten and then heard more cracks of thunder.

"A storm is coming. What do you think? Should we stay or go home?"

Patrick looked up and then he got up and crawled under the partially zipped door of the tent.

"I guess we stay," Anton said smiling.

He zipped the door open and crawled inside. He was already barefoot so he took off his shorts and shirt and lay on top of his sleeping bag. It was still pretty warm from the hot August day.

"Good night Patrick," he said hugging the dog. Patrick licked his face.

Chapter 6

It was very hot and humid, so Anton just stayed on top of his sleeping bag rather than get inside it. Patrick lay next to him and soon he was snoring. The storm got closer. Now when lightning flashed, the crack of thunder was almost instant. Patrick woke up and looked at him.

He petted the dog. "It's okay," he said quietly.

The wind began to blow in gusts. The tent began to shake as the wind buffeted it. Patrick crawled closer to him and he put his arm around the dog.

"You're safe boy," he said.

Suddenly it began to rain. There wasn't a slow sprinkle that increased, but a downpour that was like a tap was opened. The rain pounded on the tent and the sides shook as the wind gusted and blew against it. He turned on his lantern and looked to see if any water was coming in. Everything looked dry.

"Pretty scary, huh?"

Patrick looked up at him and wagged his tail.

The storm was right on top of them. Flashes of lightning made it as bright at day. Suddenly he heard a different sound on the tent. It was hailing.

"Wow," he said. "I hope this tent is strong."

The storm raged on for several minutes and then the hail stopped. Rain pelted the tent for several more minutes and then it slowed to just a light sprinkle. It was over.

"We're okay Patrick," he said.

He got up and zipped the door open. There were little piles of hail here and there where they'd collected as they ran down the sloping ground.

"Let's go see," he said crawling out.

The ground was cold on his bare feet. He walked to a pile of hail and picked up a handful. Patrick was sniffing the stuff.

He looked and the pond was much higher than it had been and there was a steady flow of water over the dam. He checked it out and saw that it was holding well.

"I guess the show is over," he said.

"Come on, let's go to bed."

They crawled into the tent. He wiped his feet off on a rag and got in his sleeping bag this time. It had cooled off a lot.

Patrick snuggled down next to him and soon they were sleeping.

Anton and Patrick were up early. They drove down to the house so they could have breakfast with his parents before they left for work. As he walked into the kitchen his mom was listening to the news on the radio.

"Morning Mom," he said.

"Morning Sweetie," she said. Then she held up her finger to let him know she was listening to something on the radio.

"Authorities are not releasing the names of those killed and injured pending the notification of relatives," the voice said. "In other news..."

"What was that?" he asked.

"There was a tornado last night about twenty miles from here," his mom said.

"Really? Someone was killed?"

She nodded. "They said three people were killed and several injured."

His dad came into the kitchen.

"Earlier they said it was an F 3 storm."

"What's that mean... F 3?"

"Well tornados are classified like earthquakes. It depends on the wind speed with tornados. There is everything from an F 0 to an F 5 tornado."

"So I suppose F 5 is the worst?"

His dad nodded. "F 0 is a storm with wind from 65 mph to 85 mph. F 1 goes from 86 mph to 110 mph. F 2 is from 111 mph to 135 and F 3 is from 136 mph to 165 mph."

"That's what the one last night was?"

His dad nodded.

"That's pretty bad huh?"

"It's bad but not as bad as an F 4 which is from 166 to 200 mph."

Anton shook his head.

"That's pretty scary."

"The worst is the F 5. Wind in an F 5 tornado is over 200 mph. They call a tornado of that strength, 'The Hand of God'."

Anton thought of two hundred miles per hour winds.

"Nothing survives an F 5," his dad said. "They take buildings, flatten forests, and anything in their path is destroyed."

"They're very rare," his mom added.

"Yes, F 5 tornados occur very seldom. But there have been some."

"Has there ever been one in Wisconsin?"

"There have been three. In 1958 there was one in Menomonie, and in 1984 one destroyed Barneveld. Then in 1996 there was one in Oakfield."

Anton knew where Barneveld was. He'd been by it last year.

"We drove by Barneveld didn't we?"

"Yes we did. Do you remember it?"

"Yeah, it wasn't very big. But it looked unusual because all of the houses were brand new. I didn't see any old houses like ours."

"That's because every house in Barneveld was destroyed. All of the buildings were flattened. The only thing left standing was the water tower."

"I remember seeing that. Wow, were people killed?"

"Yes, if I remember right there were nine people killed. There were nearly a hundred homes destroyed plus all of the businesses and buildings. The water tower was damaged but didn't topple. They found papers from some of the businesses almost a hundred and fifty miles away later."

"Wow, that's pretty scary," Anton said.

"But don't worry son," his dad said, "This old house has stood here for nearly 90 years. I think we're in a pretty safe place."

Chapter 7

That night it was still threatening to storm so Anton decided to sleep in his room. He was sitting on the porch watching the sun go down when his mom called him into the house.

"Want to watch a movie?"

"Oh I don't know. What movie?"

"The Wizard of Oz," she said.

"Is it science fiction?"

She laughed.

"No it's an old movie about a girl who goes over the rainbow. I thought with all the tornado talk, it would be a good one to watch."

"I'll pop some popcorn," his dad said.

At the word popcorn, Patrick began wagging his tail.

"See Patrick wants to watch," his dad said.

"He won't watch. He'll eat popcorn and sleep."

He shrugged.

"Sure, I'll watch it with you."

When the popcorn was done he and Patrick sat on one end of the couch with his mom on the other end. His dad was in his recliner. The movie started and Anton looked at his mom.

"How old is this movie? Where is the color?"

"The first movies were black and white. Just watch."

It didn't take long for Anton to get interested in the film. When Judy Garland sang *Somewhere over the Rainbow* he looked and saw a tear in his mom's eye.

"Why are you crying Mom?"

"That song makes me sad. She thinks her life is dull and it might be better over the rainbow, but she doesn't know it yet, she has everything she needs right there."

He didn't understand but soon the tornado came and Dorothy got sucked up into it. When the house landed, it was in Oz. The picture turned to color.

"Holy smokes, where is she?" he asked.

"She's over the rainbow honey."

Anton was mesmerized as he watched the rest of the movie, and he watched intently while Patrick lay on his back snoring.

When it was over he smiled at his parents.

"You were right, that was a good one."

"So what do you think about going over the rainbow?"

He looked down at Patrick sleeping contently.

"I'm pretty happy right here," he said.

The next morning he and Patrick filled the cooler and drove back up to the pond on the 4-wheeler. He unloaded the cooler and then the hole in the hillside popped into his head.

"Hey let's go up and look into that hole in the ground," he said.

He went into the tent and got his flashlight. They got on the 4-wheeler and drove up to the hill by the rockslide. The triangle shaped hole was gone.

"What? Where did it go?"

He walked down the hill a little way looking back and forth, thinking he was in the wrong spot. Then he decided he was right where he'd been before. He took a stick and poked at the mud bank and suddenly a bunch of mud slid away exposing the hole. It had been covered with mud and debris from the storm.

"I'm going up," he told the dog.

It was slippery and steep but after a few tries he made it up to the hole. The opening was about a foot high and a foot wide at the bottom. It was triangle shaped.

He looked in and could see it went back quite a long way. He shined the flashlight in and it really did look like a cave. The opening was filled with mud and junk but farther back he could see bare rock.

"I need some tools," he said to himself.

He and Patrick drove back down to the house. He went into the garage and grabbed a shovel, a hammer, a garden trowel and a 5gallon bucket. He looked around and didn't see anything else he might need. Then on the way out he spied a camping lantern. He looked and found a small propane tank that fit it and added those things to his tools.

"Okay Patrick, I think we can go cave exploring now," he said to the dog.

They drove back up to the cave and he carried the shovel and trowel up to the hole. It was slippery with mud and he got all covered with the stuff. Patrick worked his way up too and stood wagging his tail as Anton began shoveling mud out of the hole.

It took a lot of shoveling to get the opening cleared out. After he had the worst out he used the trowel to finish cleaning out the mud from the rainstorm.

The hole was still much too small for him to get inside.

"The sides are solid rock," he said looking at the two slabs of rock that overlapped to make the top of the triangle.

"But down here it looks like more mud than rock," he said poking at the bottom edge of the triangle. He stuck his head inside and it was two feet to the floor of the opening below the triangle.

"I think if we dig this bottom out we can get in there," he said to the dog.

Patrick was wagging his tail excitedly. He watched his master digging with the shovel and then he climbed up and began digging with his paws. The dirt was flying everywhere.

Anton laughed as he watched the dog.

"If nothing else you sure have a lot of enthusiasm Patrick," he said to the dog.

They dug for a couple of hours and made pretty good headway. The opening was now much wider at the bottom. When they cleared out the last foot or so of mud they'd be able to crawl into the first part of the cave.

Anton was getting hungry. They'd been working for a long time so he decided to call it quits for the day.

"We'll go down to the pond and wash up and then go home and get some lunch," he said.

He left the tools inside the cave and Patrick rode on the carrier and the drove to the pond. His shoes were covered with mud and so were his jeans, he took off his shirt and then he waded in wearing his shoes and jeans. Patrick jumped in and began swimming around while Anton scrubbed the mud off his jeans and shoes. Then he took them off and threw them up on the bank. He scrubbed the mud from his arms and hands and then he waded out wearing his wet boxers. Patrick was nice and clean too and the two of them drove back to the house.

Anton went up to his room and put on clean boxers and a pair of shorts. His shirt was okay so he put that on again. Then he went to the refrigerator and found some ham and cheese and made a couple of sandwiches. He and Patrick sat on the front porch and ate their lunch.

"I wonder how far that cave goes?" he said to himself. "Maybe there's some hidden treasure in there."

Patrick wagged his tail

Chapter 8

Over the next week he and Patrick cleared out the front of the cave. He dug down as far as he could until he hit rock on the bottom of the triangle too. The hole was about three feet on a side, and he could easily crawl in through it.

The room was about ten feet deep and the inside of the cave was higher and wider than the opening. At the back end of the room were another two big slabs of stone that had fallen against each other making yet another triangle shaped opening. He shined his flashlight into the room on the other side of the slabs of stone.

"This one goes a lot farther Patrick," he said. "I can't see the other end."

Patrick climbed up to the opening and looked through. He looked up at Anton like he was asking if he should go in and look at it.

"You want to see? Be careful," Anton said.

The dog crawled through the hole. Anton watched him for as long as the light carried. Then Patrick disappeared into the darkness.

He waited and the longer he waited the more he worried.

"Patrick, come on boy," he called.

His voice echoed down the cave. He waited. Patrick didn't show up.

"Patrick! Come on Patrick!"

He was getting more worried now.

Finally he heard a bark and saw Patrick's eyes glowing down in the darkness. The dog came trotting up to him and crawled through the hole. Anton hugged him.

"Dang I thought you got lost."

Patrick wagged. He wasn't worried.

For the next couple of weeks he and Patrick slept in their tent and worked on the cave opening. He took a chisel and a hammer into the hole and began chipping at the slabs of rock making the opening larger. It was slow going and he had blisters in no time.

He put the tools aside and looked at Patrick.

"Enough of this. We're going fishing and then swimming."

They did just that and the rest of the day they just lounged around on his little private beach.

He went home late in the afternoon to be with his parents. He was pretty excited about the cave but decided not to tell them about it until he got the opening made larger and could see what lay beyond it.

That night he slept in his bed at the house. It was movie night and they'd had pizza for dinner and then watched a movie and made popcorn in the evening. He kissed his folks goodnight and he and Patrick went upstairs and crawled into his bed.

It was nice sleeping in a bed instead of on an air mattress for a change but he loved his pond and his little kingdom up in the valley.

Little did he know it would be the last night he'd ever sleep in his bed.

Chapter 9

T he next day it was hot. The sun beat down on him as he climbed up to the cave. Inside it was cooler but the humidity was terrible and even in the cooler cave it was sweltering. He worked for less than an hour and he was dripping with sweat.

"Enough of this," he said. "It's too dang hot to work today Patrick. Let's go for a swim."

They drove down to the pond and he stripped off his clothes. Since he was alone in the valley he just stripped down to his birthday suit and jumped into the cool water. He and Patrick swam and played for half an hour and then he got out and lay on a blanket on the sand and dried off.

He woke a while later feeling a little sunburned. Patrick was snoring next to him.

"I need to get some clothes on or I'll turn into a lobster," he said waking the dog.

He went into the tent and got a tee shirt and some shorts and slipped them on. Then they walked up the creek a little way by a big willow tree and sat in the shade and fished for a while.

"We've got a pretty good deal going here," he said to the dog. Patrick wagged his tail and licked his hand.

He put his arm around Patrick and hugged him.

"You know I love you," he said quietly to the dog. Patrick looked into his eyes and he could see the love there too.

"I don't know what I'd do if something happened to you Patrick."

They fished and napped the rest of the day. The temperature rose and finally it was too hot even in the shade of the willow tree. They drove down to the house and turned on a fan and sat on the porch with the fan blowing on them while Anton read a book about trout fishing.

His parents came home at the usual time and they decided to cook on the grill since it was so hot in the house. They sat in the shady back yard until dusk when it was till in the upper 70 degrees.

"It's going to be a hot night," his dad said.

"I think I'll sleep at the pond."

"Are you sure Honey? You could bring your sleeping bag up here and sleep in our room. We have the only AC in there."

"I'll sleep down there. It's cooler by the water. Patrick and I have slept there most of the summer. I'll be fine."

His mom hugged him and kissed him on the cheek. His dad gave him a hug and he waved as he walked out the door.

"Dang, I've got the best parents in the world," he thought to himself. "I'm a lucky kid."

Anton lay on top of his sleeping bag on the grass outside his tent. It was dark so the mosquitoes had gone to bed and it was a little cooler out there. Soon a slight breeze began to blow from the west.

Patrick lay on his side snoring. Suddenly he raised his head and looked to the west.

"Can you hear something?"

Anton looked west and saw a little flash of light a long way off. He sat up and watched and soon there was another flash and then another.

"It's gonna storm," he said.

The storm looked like it was a big one. Soon there was lightning all the way across the horizon. The flashes were non-stop.

"It's a big storm Patrick," he said.

The dog sat next to him as if he was worried.

"It'll be okay boy."

The air became deadly calm. The humidity was so thick you could hardly breathe. The air actually felt charged like it had electricity in it.

The storm got closer and closer. The lightning cracked and the thunder boomed. He and Patrick crawled inside the tent and zipped it up tight. He could see out the window and watched the storm.

"Maybe we should have made a run for home," he said. But he knew the storm was close and now it was too late to run for shelter.

Then he heard the sound. He couldn't figure out what it was. There was a roaring noise, like a big truck was passing, or maybe a train.

The wind suddenly began to whip back and forth and the trees bent over. The tent began to shake and rattle. Then there was a flash of lightning and he saw it.

"Oh my God Patrick, it's a tornado!"

The funnel cloud was coming right up the valley floor. It was at least as wide as the whole valley and everything in its path was being torn from the ground and hurled up into the air.

The noise was deafening. Branches and dirt slammed into the tent. He saw a wagon that had been parked down by the house, fly past. Then his dirt bike tipped onto its side and was gone.

"Patrick!" he yelled as he grabbed the dog.

The tent lifted off the ground and they were up in the air.

Patrick was yelping and Anton was screaming in terror.

They spun and he didn't know how high they were but he knew... they were being picked up by the tornado.

It seemed like an hour but it was probably only a few seconds that he was off he ground. Suddenly the tent ripped in half and was gone. He was holding onto Patrick waiting to hit the ground. He had his arms wrapped tightly around the dog.

The wind spun him around. Something slammed into his back. There was a searing pain shooting down his back to his legs. He flew and twisted and had no idea which way was up. Then something slammed into his arm and then to his horror, he lost his grip on the dog. Patrick was yelping and he was holding onto one of his legs. Suddenly the leg slipped from his grip. Patrick disappeared into the darkness.

"Patrick! Patrick!" he screamed.

Patrick was gone.

He was screaming and crying and suddenly all the terror and noise stopped. He was falling. He hit the ground with a thud, and his vision darkened. He had been thrown out of the wind stream and had landed in the lower end of the pasture in the swampy part of the field. He was knocked out cold.

Chapter 10

It was still very dark. There was a light rain falling. Anton slowly came from the darkness and opened his eyes. He had no idea where he was or how he got there.

He hurt everywhere. He raised his head and the pain in his neck nearly made him pass out. He lay his head back down in the soft earth. The rain felt good on his face.

"What happened?" he thought.

"How did I get here? Where is this place?"

He closed his eyes again and tried to remember. Slowly it came back to him. The tornado! He'd been sucked up into it!

"Oh God! Patrick!"

He tried to raise his head again and the pain was terrible. He turned to the side and all he could see was short grass and mud.

"It's wet here, I must be in the lower pasture where the swamp is."

He moved his left arm and it seemed to be okay. He tried to lift his right arm and he couldn't do it. There was a terrible pain in the elbow. Then he tried to sit up.

Nothing.

He tried again to sit up. He couldn't move.

"What's wrong with me?" he said out loud.

He tried again and then he realized. He couldn't feel his legs. All he could feel was his left arm. He was paralyzed.

"Oh God, please help me," he prayed.

He lay there for several minutes and called to Patrick. He was so tired. He tried to stay awake but he just couldn't do it.

As dawn broke Anton woke up again. He looked right and left and knew he was in the pasture down in the valley. He could see the hills off to his right.

"Patrick!"

He expected to hear the dog running to him. Nothing.

"Patrick! Here boy!"

Nothing.

"I must have hurt something in my back or legs," he thought. "Mom and Dad will be here looking for me soon."

But no one came. The sun rose and the temperature warmed up. The sky was bright blue with just a few little fluffy clouds passing over him.

No one came. He called for Patrick every few minutes. Nothing.

He was lying in the soft marsh of the upper part of the valley. His back was in water and it was very cold.

"Someone has to come soon," he thought. "They have to."

He went back to unconsciousness.

Hours later he heard a voice. He listened and then he heard another.

"Check that low spot," someone said.

He heard footsteps.

"I'm here! I'm here!" he yelled.

"Over here, I've got someone alive."

A man came hurrying over by him. He knelt in the wet mud. He was wearing one of those little bright orange vests over a uniform

"Are hurt son?"

"I can't move my legs," he said.

"Just stay calm. We're here to help you."

The man called on a little radio and in a few minutes there were several more people there. They were all wearing orange vests over their outer clothes.

"Was anyone with you son?"

"Patrick was with me. I've called and called and he's not coming."

The man looked at one of the others.

"Who is Patrick?"

"He's my dog. He's a beagle."

The man looked sad and shook his head.

"What? Have you found Patrick?"

"Let's get you out of here, then we'll see about that," the man said.

"I want to know. Tell me. Where is he?"

A lady knelt down by him.

"Sweetie, Patrick didn't make it. We found him. He's gone. I'm so sorry."

Anton's eyes filled with tears. Right then he didn't care if they carried him out of there or not. His best friend was gone.

"Patrick is dead? No it can't be."

He felt a ringing in his ears and got dizzy. Then the light faded and he went to a dark place.

When Anton woke again he was in a hospital bed. He looked around and there was a nurse a little way away by a machine. She saw him awake and hurried over to him.

"Hello. How are you feeling?"

He looked at her. How did she think he felt? How did anyone feel when his best friend was dead? He didn't answer.

"I'll get the doctor." She hurried off.

A few minutes later a man came in wearing a white coat. He looked at Anton and checked the machines.

"Hello young man."

Anton looked at him.

"I'm Dr. Andrews. You've had quite a hard night."

He lay there looking up. He really had nothing to say. His insides felt empty.

"You have a broken right arm, and you cracked three vertebrae. There is a lot of swelling in your back and the swelling has pinched your spinal cord. That's why you can't feel your legs."

He said nothing.

"Otherwise you have a lot of bruises and scrapes. But overall you came through the tornado pretty well. Not many survive a storm like that."

The nurse smiled at him.

"Can we get you anything sweetie?"

He shook his head.

A man walked up behind the doctor. It was Father James from his church. The doctor and the priest conferred in low voices and then the priest moved up by the bed.

"Hello Anton," he said.

Anton looked at him but didn't answer.

"I'm so sorry for all of the terrible things that have happened to you son."

He stood there as if he didn't want to go on. He reached down and took Anton's good hand and held it.

"I have bad news son. There's no way to say this so it will be easy. Your parents didn't survive the tornado. I'm sorry Anton, they're both gone."

His head swam and his ears rang and he closed his eyes. Tears squeezed out under his eyelids and ran down his cheeks. His mom was gone. His dad was gone. Patrick was gone.

He wished he were gone too.

Two Years Later...

Chapter 11

P aul Daniels carried the first box into his new room. He sat it on the floor and looked around. He was happy his family had finally been able to settle down and build this new house. They'd been moving from one Army base to another for all of his sixteen years. Now his dad had retired and they were finally going to stay in one place for a while.

"Is it okay?" his mom asked as she walked into the room.

"Mom it's perfect. I've never had such a nice room."

He hugged his mom. She had been such a great mom through all the moves when his dad had been moved to the places the army needed him to be. She'd always been there for him.

"Not a bad barracks," his dad said as he carried a box into the room.

"It's perfect Dad. You built everything I wanted into it. I couldn't ask for more."

"Well we've been in some pretty awful places so this time we decided to build a house instead of buy one that wasn't exactly what we wanted. This move is our last one. My job at the college is permanent and your mom's job at the hospital is just as stable so we're here for good."

"I'm glad. Maybe this time I can make some friends that I actually can spend a few years with," Paul said.

Paul favored his father in looks. His dad a big strapping guy who stood two inches over six feet tall. Paul was exactly that and he had just turned sixteen. Both had medium brown hair, brown eyes and an easy smile. His dad had been a Colonel in the army and was a smart guy. Paul was a straight A student so he took after him in intelligence too.

He inherited his mom's easy-going way and her sense of humor. His mom was a fun lady who loved to prank him whenever she got the chance.

The house they were moving into was built on the land of an old farm that had been destroyed two years earlier by a tornado. All of the buildings had been flattened and a five hundred foot swath of trees had been flattened as the storm swept over the ridge behind the farmhouse. The people who lived in the house were killed and their son was hospitalized still. He didn't know much about them but felt bad that they'd died on this spot.

The house had everything they'd wanted and was built to their specifications. They had a big hot tub in back on their expansive patio. The back patio was like an outdoor kitchen with a huge grill, refrigerator, and all the goodies for summer cooking in the outdoors. His dad was a grilling maniac.

Paul arranged his stuff in his dresser and closet and looked over the room. He couldn't be happier with it. Now if he could find some new friends at this school, he'd really be happy.

Paul's mom, Nancy was a registered nurse and found a job at the hospital and nursing home in town. The hospital had a wing dedicated to older people who needed help and for people who were recovering from surgeries or accidents or people who needed nursing care.

The head nurse was taking her on a tour of the place showing her how everything worked. They went through the hospital wing and then to the nursing facility. She met several of the residents and they all were happy to see her.

They went by one small room and the head nurse took her

inside. A young boy was sitting looking out the window. He was slim and had dark hair that was lighter in front, and brown eyes and a very sweet face.

"Anton, this is Nancy. She will be one of our new nurses."

The boy looked up. His eyes looked dead. He didn't say anything but turned back to the window.

Nancy looked at the other nurse and she motioned to the hall.

"We call him the boy who fell from the sky," She said. "His family lived where you now live. His name is Anton and he's fifteen. Two years ago there was a terrible tornado. His parents and his dog were killed but he survived. He had several broken bones and a broken back but with a lot of care he's physically fine now.

"Can he speak?"

"Physically he has no reason not to speak. When he found out his parents and his dog were dead he shut down. He's not spoken a word since."

Nancy looked in the doorway. Her heart nearly broke.

"Why is he here?"

"He has no living relatives. We've tried to get him into foster care but with his speaking situation no one will take him."

"Is he hostile? Doe he act-out?"

"He is as sweet as he can be. He does as he's told but is non-communicative. He just refuses to speak."

They moved on to the rest of the place but all the while, the image of Anton sitting by the window haunted Nancy. There had to be something that could be done for him.

Chapter 12

"I saw a boy at the nursing home today that used to live here," she said that night at dinner.

"He lived here?"

"Yes right here where our home is. He lived in the old farmhouse with his parents."

"But why is he at the nursing home?" Chuck, Paul's dad asked.

"They call him the boy who fell from the sky. They say he was sucked up in the tornado and carried several hundred yards down the valley. He fell from the tornado and luckily landed in a marsh where the ground was very soft. He survived the tornado but everyone else was killed including his dog. He has no living relatives so the county sold the land, which we bought, and put the money into a trust for him. He was hurt very badly in the tornado but he's better now. His problem is that he doesn't speak."

"He can't or won't?" Paul asked.

"When he found out his parents and his dog were dead he stopped speaking. He hasn't said a word in two years."

"Holy cow."

She explained that no one would take him in the foster care program and for now he was living with a bunch of elderly people.

"That can't be good," Paul's dad said.

"No it's not good. I wish we could help him."

Paul and his dad looked at her.

"You mean like take him in?"

"I mean maybe we could invite him out for a day to see the new place. I don't know. I feel so bad for him. He's a sweet little guy."

That night Paul lay in bed and he was thinking about the boy in the nursing home. It must have been horrible to lose his family and survive and be alone.

"I should talk to Mom and see if I can help," he thought to himself.

The next morning he told his mom he would like to see if he could do something for the kid.

"I'll talk to the head nurse and see what she thinks," his mom said.

At noon he was making a sandwich when his phone rang. It was his mom.

"Honey, they think it's worth a try to see if he might respond to a boy his own age. Why don't you drive to town this afternoon and we'll see what happens?"

He told his mom he'd be there at about 1 o'clock.

Paul was a little lost. The hospital was a big place and he didn't know for sure where to go. He was wandering down one hall when he saw his mom talking to a man in a white lab coat. She saw him and motioned for him to come.

"Paul this is Dr. Laurent. Dr. this is my son Paul."

They shook hands.

"So you're going to try to get through to Anton," the doctor said.

"Well I thought I'd see if he might respond to someone his own age. I don't know what will happen but I'm willing to try," Paul said.

"That's all any one can do," he said. "Physically he's fine. He's just so sad that he has shut down and will not speak to anyone. We've tried everything with no results, so don't be disappointed if he doesn't respond."

His mom took him to the dining room. The residents had just finished eating and the nurses were taking them back to their rooms. She pointed to the corner where the boy was sitting by himself at a table. His dishes were empty but he just sat looking at the table.

"His name is Anton. He's just a little younger than you. I have no idea if he'll be receptive to you. If he's not just let it go."

Paul nodded. He walked across the room. The kid was a little smaller than he was and quite thin. His dark hair was longish in front and lighter colored and his brown eyes looked very sad. Paul smiled as he walked up and the kid looked up at him. He made no response.

"Hi, I'm Paul," he said. "Do you mind it I sit down?"

Anton followed him with his eyes but made no response.

Paul sat down.

"How's the food here?"

No response.

"My mom is Nancy, she's the new nurse."

There was a spark of something as he said that.

"He understands," Paul thought.

"Mom told me you had a bad deal a while ago. I'm sorry to hear that. It must be terrible."

Anton's eyes blinked several times.

"My dad was in the army for twenty years. He's out now and teaching at the university. We built a house on the land where you used to live."

Anton's eyes widened. He was interested.

"You had a really cool place. I love that valley. I bet you had a lot of cool places to explore and stuff."

Anton's eyes looked excited.

47

"I haven't looked around too much but I'd sure like it if you could come out and show me around."

He looked at the kid and Paul could tell he was thinking.

"I was wondering if you might like to come out to the place with me someday and show me all the cool stuff. The Doctor said it would be okay."

Just then one of the ladies from the nursing home clapped her hands and started laughing. They both turned and a woman was leading a golden retriever into the dining room. The residents were all petting the dog and talking to it.

Paul looked at Anton and he was fascinated as he watched. He liked the dog. His eyes sparkled as the dog went from resident to resident getting petted. It was one of those therapy dogs that people took to places like this so the residents could have contact with a dog.

"Be right back," he said.

He walked to the other side of the room.

"Could you bring her over there? That boy is very interested in her. He hasn't spoken in two years."

The lady called the dog to follow her and they walked over by Anton.

He looked very excited as the dog came to him and lay it's head in his lap. He smiled as he petted the soft fur.

Paul looked at his mom and she smiled at him widely.

"What's the dog's name?" he asked.

"Her name is Taffy," the lady said.

"Hear that Anton, the dog's name is Taffy."

Anton looked up at him and smiled.

Chapter 13

"The dog is the secret to him getting better," he told his mom later. "When he saw it he just brightened right up. You said his dog was killed in the tornado?"

"Yes, he and the dog were camping and they were actually swept up in the thing I'm told. He survived but the dog didn't. He loved his dog more than anything."

The next day Paul went back to the nursing home. He found Anton in his room, sitting and looking out the window.

"Hey, how is it going?" Paul asked as he stood in the doorway.

Anton looked up at him and there was a slight smile on his face.

"Is it okay if I come in?"

Anton nodded slightly.

"I was wondering if you'd like to get out of here for a while and go to the park with me?"

Anton's eyes looked excited but he didn't say anything.

"I'm going to ask the Doc and if he says it's okay well go."

Paul talked to the Doctor and told him of Anton's interest in the dog. He said by all means to take him out.

When Paul got back to the room Anton was standing by the door waiting.

"Ready to go?"

Anton didn't say anything but he stepped right up and Paul could tell he was happy to get out of there.

They went out and got in the car and Paul drove down by the river to the park. Anton looked out the window and watched everything go by.

"It must be boring in that place with all those old people," Paul said. "I mean, it's not their fault that they're old but they can't be much fun to be with."

Anton looked at him with a slight smile.

They pulled up at the park and got out. They walked along the river and Paul talked. He tried to get the kid to answer him many times but all he got was a look.

They went a while and soon they saw a young guy with a black lab. The guy was throwing a stick out into the river and the dog was swimming out and retrieving it. Anton was mesmerized.

"Cool dog," Paul said.

Anton nodded.

They walked up to the guy and watched. The dog came back with the stick and dropped it and then shook off. He filled the air with water and they all got a little wet. Anton was actually smiling.

"Can he throw it?" Paul asked, motioning to Anton.

The guy handed the stick to him. He stood there for a minute and then he threw it into the river.

"Fetch Romeo," the guy said and the dog leaped into the river.

Anton watched and when the dog got back he dropped the stick at Anton's feet. He reached down and looked at the guy.

"Go ahead throw it again," he said.

Paul motioned for the guy to move off a little.

"He was nearly killed a couple of years ago and his dog was killed with his parents. He hasn't talked since. This is the most I've seen him do."

"He sure likes the dog," the guy said.

"No kidding. I think a dog is the secret to getting him back among the living."

"Anton's dog was a beagle," Paul's mom said when she got home that evening.

"A beagle. I wonder if anyone around here has any beagles for sale?" Paul asked.

"Check on the Internet or the newspaper," his dad suggested.

Paul searched and searched. The only beagles he found were just four weeks old and were in a town about twenty miles away. The owner was taking deposits on them for when they were ready to go to their new homes.

Paul called the man.

"How many pups do you have?" he asked.

"We've got seven but three are spoken for already."

"Are any of the ones left males?"

"Yes two are males."

Paul explained to the man about Anton and how he thought it might get him out of his silent mood if he had a dog to care for.

"You bring the boy over and we'll work it out," the man said.

"Can I take Anton on a field trip?"

"I think it could be arranged. What are you planning Honey?"

Paul explained the puppies and his mom and dad were all for the plan. He went to bed that night with high hopes.

The next day Paul arrived at the nursing home just before lunch. His mom had arranged for him to eat there. The residents were seated and eating. Anton sat alone at his table with his tray.

Paul carried a tray of food across the room and stopped at Anton's table.

"Can I join you?"

Anton looked up surprised but when he saw Paul he nearly smiled.

Paul sat and looked at the food.

"Well this looks pretty... I'm not sure what it is."

Anton smiled slightly.

Paul took a bite of a casserole and it wasn't half bad.

"Hmm, not as bad as it looks," he said grinning.

They ate silently for a while.

"Hey, you seem to know a lot about dogs. I saw the way that dog went right to you the other day. I'm thinking about getting a new dog. I was wondering if you might like to go with me and help me pick one out?"

Anton looked excited. He didn't speak but his eyes said yes.

"I talked to the head nurse and she said you can go with me as long as we're back by dinner time."

Anton's head nodded... barely.

They finished eating and walked to Anton's room. He was wearing slippers and changed into sneakers. Then they walked out and got into Paul's car.

"Well this should be fun. I've wanted a dog for a long time but when you're in the military you move all the time and they frown on dogs on base. So now that I'm here permanently my folks said I can get one."

Anton nodded again.

They drove to the town where the puppies were and Paul got lost a couple of times but finally they found the place. Anton jumped out of the car and was excited as they walked up to the house. They knocked and a man came to the door.

"I'm Paul, I'm the guy who called about the puppy."

"Carl," the man said.

"This is Anton. He's more knowledgeable about dogs than I am. He's going to help me pick one out." Paul winked and the man understood.

"Well they're all out back in the yard."

They walked through the house and when the man opened

the door there were seven beagle puppies and the mother dog all playing in the grass. Paul stepped out and looked at Anton who was stopped in his tracks.

"Are you okay?" he said taking Anton's arm.

He looked at the dogs and then at Paul. He nodded. His eyes were moist. He blinked several times. Then a big tear ran down his cheek. He blinked several more times and then wiped his face with his shirtsleeve.

They walked out and Anton knelt down and soon he had a lapful of puppies. They climbed over him and some were tugging at his shoelaces. One climbed up and was licking his chin. His face was glowing.

"I think he likes them," Carl said quietly.

"I've never seen him smile like this," Paul said. "This is just what he needs."

Paul joined Anton on the ground and they played with the puppies for half an hour. Eventually the pups got tired and all soon ended up in the shade in a big pile and they took a nap.

"What do you think? Do you think any of them would make a good dog for me?"

Anton looked at him and nodded eagerly.

"Those with little ribbons on them are already spoken for," Carl said.

"I think I'd like a male," Paul said and Anton nodded.

"Those two right there are the males that are left."

They looked at the two little pups. One was almost all black and brown and the other was black and brown with some white around his neck and on his face.

"Which one?" Paul asked.

Anton pointed to the one with the white markings.

"Okay I'll take that one," he said to the man.

"They need about another week with their mama. I'll start weaning them in a few days. Then when they get used to dog food you can come and pick him up."

He tied a purple ribbon on the dog's neck.

"I guess we have to wait a few days," Paul said.

Anton nodded. He reached down and picked up the puppy and held it to his chest. He hugged the little dog and tears ran from his eyes. Paul felt his eyes tearing up too.

"Patrick."

Paul looked surprised. "What did you say?"

"Patrick."

Anton spoke. He said the name Patrick.

"You want to call him Patrick?"

Anton nodded.

"Patrick it is."

Anton held the pup and cried. Paul and Carl walked a little way off.

"That's the first word he's spoken in two years," Paul said quietly.

"The dog is yours."

"What?"

"The dog is yours or his, whichever. I can't ask you to pay for that dog. That was quite an experience for me to see that boy come back to the world. I'll never forget that."

"Then give it to him, not me."

Carl smiled and walked over to Anton.

"Son that puppy is yours now. As soon as he's ready to go home, I want you to have him for your own."

Anton looked surprised and then he smiled widely.

"Thank you!"

Chapter 14

Paul didn't know what to do. He was so excited about Anton speaking and he didn't know if he should press him to talk some more. Finally he decided to try a conversation.

"Dang those puppies were cute," he said.

Anton nodded.

"I'm glad you were along. I wouldn't have known which one to choose."

Anton smiled.

"I like the name Patrick."

Anton turned to him.

"My other dog was Patrick."

Holy crap, five words.

"That's nice that you named this one Patrick also. It's like to honor him."

Anton' eyes got wet. He looked out the window a minute.

"I tried to keep him safe and I failed."

"Oh it wasn't your fault. I heard that the tornado was huge and very powerful."

"I should have held him tighter."

Paul didn't know for sure what to say.

"I'm really sorry you lost him."

Anton nodded.

"He spoke?"

"He named the dog then he told the guy 'thank you' and on the way home we actually had a conversation."

"Paul you should be a therapist," his mom said hugging him.

"I've got to talk to the doctors. They're going to be so happy."

"Um Mom, the dog has to stay there for about a week. He's not weaned yet. But, the man gave him to Anton. He won't be able to have a dog here, will he?"

"Oh that would be against the rules. Visiting dogs are okay but not resident dogs."

"So now what?"

She looked at him and she knew he had already figured it out.

"Are you sure?"

Paul smiled. "What?"

"You're thinking he should come and stay with us."

Paul smiled widely.

"That did cross my mind."

"Do you want another boy to share your stuff?"

"Why have stuff if you can't share?"

His mom hugged him.

"I have the most wonderful son in the world," she said.

"So he can come?"

"I'll talk to the doctors and social services. And we have to see if it's okay with your dad."

"It will be, you know that."

"Yes it will be. Well I guess if all the proper people say it's okay, then it's okay with me too."

He beamed.

"He's a nice kid. He's very sad and withdrawn but I think I can be friends with him and he'll be fine."

"Don't say anything to him until we're sure," his mom warned.

"We have to go visit Patrick tomorrow. He wants to make sure he's okay."

She smiled.

"Patrick?"

Paul nodded. "Now you have three sons, Paul, Anton and Patrick."

Chapter 15

Anton was waiting by the front door when Paul pulled into the hospital. He came running out with a big smile on his face.

"Hi," Paul said.

"Hi," Anton replied.

"Are you excited to see Patrick?"

Anton nodded.

They took off down the road.

"I wonder if he'll remember us?" Paul said.

Anton nodded and smiled.

He was better but still not real chatty. That was okay with Paul as long as they made progress.

They arrived at the house and Carl was waiting to see them. The dogs were in the back yard like they'd been the day before.

Anton couldn't get back there fast enough. Paul and Carl held back and let him go out into the yard on his own.

He went right to the little pup and picked him up. Patrick began licking him excitedly. He turned and beamed at Paul and Carl.

"He likes me," he said.

"That he does lad," Carl said.

Anton got down in the grass and soon he was in the middle

of a pile of puppies. He rolled around with them and he was as happy as any boy ever could be.

"That little dog has changed his life," Paul said.

"Isn't that something? Two years of silence and now look at him," Carl replied.

"That was a nice thing for you to give him the pup."

"I didn't breed these puppies to make money. I did it because a friend loves my old girl there and he begged me to get a pup from her. The look on that boy's face is payment enough."

Paul joined Anton on the ground and they had a great time with the puppies. After a while the pups got tired and all lay in a pile for a nap.

Paul's phone vibrated and he answered it. He listened for a minute. Then he smiled widely.

"I'll see if he wants to do that," he said and hung up.

Anton looked at him.

"That was my mom. She talked to the doctors and the social services people. When she told them about Patrick they said that you would have to live someplace else besides the nursing home because they don't allow people to have dogs there. They think it would be a good thing for you to go to a foster home now that you're all better."

"A foster home?"

"Yeah, live with a family and be a part of that family."

"I don't know anyone."

"You know me and my mom."

Suddenly he got it.

"You mean with you?"

Paul nodded. "And of course Patrick will come too."

Anton blinked a few times and then he leaned forward and tentatively put his arms around Paul.

Paul grabbed him and hugged him hard.

"Thank you," Anton whispered.

In the doorway, Carl wiped his eyes with a sleeve.

When they got back to the nursing home it seemed that everyone knew of the news. They were all smiling and saying goodbye to Anton. He seemed a little overwhelmed at it all.

They packed up his stuff, which wasn't much and he and Paul headed for his new home.

As they pulled out of the parking lot he looked back and wiped his eyes.

"They were nice to me there. But it's not the place for someone my age."

"The next part of your life is starting right now," Paul said.

Anton smiled at him.

"I'm ready."

Chapter 16

As they turned down the lane that went to Paul's house, Anton was visibly agitated. He seemed to get more and more tense as they got to the valley. When Paul turned around the last turn Paul could see he was on the verge of crying.

Paul stopped the car.

"It looks a lot different now," he said quietly.

Anton nodded. His eyes were filled with tears.

"We can go back or wait a while," Paul said. "I know it has to be hard to see it now with everything different."

Anton shook his head.

"Let's go."

They drove up to the new house. It was sitting exactly where the old one had been. Paul hadn't seen the old place but his dad told him that everything had been destroyed except the foundation of the old house. The garage was gone, the shed was gone and the house was gone. The tornado had erased the whole place.

Anton got out of the car and stood there looking around.

"All gone," he said.

"This is the first time you've been here?"

He nodded.

"After it happened I had a broken back. I had to be in a bed for almost eight weeks. I couldn't move. I didn't even get to go to my parents funeral."

Paul put his arm around the boy's shoulder.

"I'm sorry for all your troubles," he said.

"One of the firemen told me they found my dog and buried him by my pond."

"You had a pond?"

Anton nodded and pointed up the valley. "Patrick and I built it."

"Let's go see."

They got in the car and drove up the pasture. Anton pointed toward a spot where the valley was flat and wide and they stopped. There was a patch of sand in the middle of a bunch of weeds and what was left of a rock dam in the creek.

Anton walked down by the creek.

"This was our dam. That whole place there was a pond," he said pointing to a wide spot in the creek.

"You built that all?"

He nodded. "Patrick and I had a tent up here. We'd sleep here and go fishing and swimming. We were in the tent when the... when it happened."

Paul looked around and it was really a nice place. There was a rope hanging from a big branch on a maple tree across the creek.

"Did you swing on that?"

Anton nodded.

Then Paul spotted a wooden cross next to a willow tree a little way up the bank of the creek.

"Look," he said.

Anton saw the cross and they walked up. Someone had taken two pieces of wood and nailed them together and stuck them in the ground beneath the tree.

Anton knelt down in the grass and touched the ground by the cross. His eyes filled with tears.

"Hello Patrick. I've missed you," he said. "I'm sorry I didn't take better care of you that night."

Paul felt like his heart was breaking. He squatted down by the boy and hugged his shoulder.

"You did the best you could Anton. Patrick was lucky to have you as his friend."

Anton nodded.

"Why don't we re-build it?"

Anton looked over at him.

"The pond?"

"Yeah, the two of us can build it back up and clean up the place. I love to camp and fish. If you don't mind sharing your spot, I'd love to help."

The boy smiled.

"That'd be good."

Chapter 17

"So if we could find a good used 4-wheeler it'd be really good," Paul explained at the dinner table that evening. His dad and mom were listening to his plea for the vehicle and Anton sat watching.

"So that's how you built the old dam?" Paul's dad asked.

"Yes sir. I had a rack on the back and hauled rocks down from the hill. I also had some timbers and boards that I found on the old farm. Some of the rocks are in the stream below the old dam but we'd need more to do it right."

Paul's mom smiled at his dad.

"Wouldn't it be nice to have a pond? Just think you could go up there and catch dinner some time."

"It would only take a thousand trout to pay for the 4-wheeler too," his dad said grinning.

"We could use it for other chores too. We need to get some firewood put up for winter so we can use our fireplace. Anton and I can do that with the vehicle too."

"I'll stop tomorrow and see what they have," his dad said.

The boys beamed.

They helped with the dishes and then the whole family sat on the porch until dark. The mosquitoes were starting to bother so they went inside.

"I'm heading to bed," Paul said. "We've got a big day tomorrow."

"Good night boys," his parents said.

Anton hesitated and then walked over to the parents.

"Thank you for letting me come here," he said.

He hugged both of them.

Paul and Anton went to his room. His parents had moved in a second bed for Anton. The room was quite large so it didn't bother at all to have a second bed.

"We'll have to get you some more clothes and stuff," Paul said looking at the little amount of stuff in the new dresser by Anton's bed. "Mom said we could stop and get some stuff on the way back from visiting Patrick tomorrow."

Anton smiled when he said that.

"Can Patrick sleep in here with us?"

"I don't see why not. Of course if he pees, you have to clean it up."

"No problem."

They both undressed to their boxers and got into their beds. Paul shut the light off.

"Paul?"

"Yeah?"

"Thank you."

"For what Anton?"

"For helping me come back... for Patrick... for letting me have half your room. For a lot of stuff."

"Hey it's no problem. I've moved around all my life and never really got to be friends with anyone for any long period of time. I've always wanted a best friend."

"You mean me?"

"Of course."

There was a long pause.

"I never thought I could be happy again," he said. "When everyone I loved was taken away, I really didn't want to live. Many times when I was lying with my broken back I just wished I'd go to sleep and never wake up."

"But life goes on Anton."

"Yeah, I guess so. But at that time I didn't think it would."

Paul threw back the covers and got up and walked over to Anton's bed. He sat on the side of it.

"Listen, what happened is over. From now on you have a new family that loves you. My parents both were all for bringing you here. I was all for it too. We want you to be a part of our family. I want you to be my brother."

Anton blinked back some tears. He sat up in the bed and put his arms around Paul.

"Thank you brother," he whispered.

Chapter 18

P aul sat down at the breakfast table with his parents.
"Where is Anton?" his mom asked.
"He was just finishing up in the shower. He'll be here in a minute," he said.

"Paul you've done a wonderful job getting him to open up again," his mom said. "The doctors are just thrilled at his progress."

"It wasn't me so much as the dog that got him talking again. I just happened to see how he responded to that dog in the hospital and put it together."

"Well you've been a great friend to him," his dad said.

"He's a nice kid. Actually it's nice for me too. I don't know any of the kids here so I have someone to hang with too."

Just then Anton walked into the kitchen wearing his tee shirt and shorts, his hair still wet.

"You guys should go shopping today and get Anton some new clothes," his mom suggested.

"I'll work for some money to buy some," the boy said.

"Don't worry about that Sweetie. We'll get plenty of work out of you when you and Paul start making firewood for the winter."

"Can we use a chain saw?"

Paul's dad grinned. "Typical boy."

The parents left for work and the boys decided to go to town and shop. Paul's mom had given him her credit card so they had plenty of money. They drove to Walmart first for the basics. Anton needed underwear and socks for cooler weather, and some tee shirts. They also bought a few pair of shorts and a pair of flip-flops. As the wandered through the store they came past the sporting goods department. Anton stopped at a stack of tents on a shelf.

"We should get one of those," Paul said.

"I don't know," Anton said quietly.

"Anton, what happened was one in a million. That old farmhouse stood there for nearly a hundred years. The odds of another tornado coming down our valley are nearly impossible."

"Yeah, I guess so."

"It's okay. We don't need one. I just thought it would be fun to camp by the pond when we get it re-built."

"So we're really going to re-build it?"

"Just as soon as Dad gets a 4-wheeler for us. He's been looking at them. He tried to find a good used one but I think he's going for a new one now."

"Then let's get a tent," the boy said smiling.

They looked them over and decided on one that was big enough for them and Patrick to have plenty of room. Then they bought two air mattresses and two sleeping bags, a lantern, a cooler and some folding chairs and a little camp table.

"Your mom is gonna poop when she sees this bill," Anton said grinning.

"She'll get over it."

They checked out and went to another store where they bought Anton some jeans and a light jacket. Then he picked out a pair of sneakers and a pair of leather work-boots.

The next stop was Taco Bell.

"Are we going to visit Patrick today?" Anton asked as he shoved the last of a taco into his mouth.

"We might as well as long as we're in town anyway," Paul said.

They drove to Patrick's house and Carl was smiling widely

when they drove up.

"I think today is the day," he said.

"What? Can he come home with us today?" Anton asked excitedly.

"He's been eating Puppy Chow like a madman. I think he knows it's a ticket out of here. Three of the other pups have already left for their new homes."

Anton had a wide grin on his face as he walked out into the back yard. The puppy looked up and saw him and came running. He got ahead of himself and tipped over on his nose half way there. Anton was on the ground when he got to him and scooped him up and kissed his little face.

Carl looked at Paul and nodded.

"This is a good thing," he said quietly.

"Thanks Carl. He'll never forget you for this."

Carl got the papers for Patrick and they thanked him again. Anton hugged the man and Carl's eyes got wet.

"You two stop and see me sometime," he said.

"We will, I promise," Anton said.

Carl hugged the boy and then hugged the little dog.

"You be a good boy," he said to the little pup.

On the way home Patrick sat in Anton's lap and looked out the window. He was fascinated at all the wonderful things going past.

"Just look at how alert he is. You can tell he's really smart," Anton said beaming.

"Smart as a whip," Paul said. "Smart as a whip."

Chapter 19

"We better stop at Walmart again and get some Puppy Chow for him," Paul said.

Anton agreed but stayed in the car with the puppy.

Paul went in and bought a bag of dog food and then he bought a little dog bed and a pair of food bowls. Then he stopped and got a dog ball and a tug-of-war dog rope. He picked up a canvas duck too.

When he got back in the car Anton motioned for him to be quiet. Patrick was lying on his back in his lap sleeping.

"He's really tired," the boy said.

Paul smiled as they drove off toward home. That little dog was going to be the thing that would bring Anton back to the world and it was going to be fun to be a part of that.

When they pulled into the driveway Anton took Patrick out and put him in the grass so he could go potty. The puppy sprinted around for a minute and then squatted and peed.

Anton looked at Paul with a concerned look on his face.

"Old Patrick used to lift his leg and pee. New Patrick pees like a girl."

Paul laughed.

"I think they squat until they get a little bigger. There's nothing wrong with him."

"You think?"

"He's all boy. Give him a few weeks and he'll be peeing like a boy all over the place."

They went inside and hauled all the stuff into the house. It took several trips and while they hauled, Patrick explored. By the time they had everything from the car the little guy had pulled three rugs into the living room and had seven shoes piled up with them. He was laying on top of his little pile of treasures wagging his tail.

"I think he likes it here," Anton said looking down at the little guy.

"He's been busy while we were working. We're going to have to put stuff up until he gets over that collecting habit."

They took Patrick into their bedroom. Paul showed Anton the little dog bed and the toys. Anton put the bed right next to his on the floor and then began playing with him with the toys.

Paul took the tags off the new clothes and helped put them into a dresser.

"We're home," came the call from the front of the house. "What's with all these rugs and shoes?"

They walked to the living room and Patrick skated across the slippery wood floor behind them. His mom and dad looked a bit surprised when they saw him.

"Oh my we have a new little person in the house," Paul's mom said.

She got down on the floor and soon Patrick was in her lap licking her face. Paul's dad watched and smiled.

"Look at the smile on that boy's face," he said quietly as they looked at Anton watching the dog.

"You'd never know he was silent and non-responsive just a short time ago," Paul said.

"You did good when you figured that dog thing out."

Paul shrugged. "Lucky guess."

They saw the pile of camping gear on the floor inside the door and Paul explained that they were going to use it once the pond was re-built. He gave his mom her credit card and the receipt for all the stuff. Her eyes widened when she was the total but hen she smiled and nodded. It was worth it to see how Anton was now acting compared to the little quiet boy he'd been.

As they sat around the dinner table Paul's dad asked if they were going to be home the next day.

"We should be."

"I'm having something delivered at about noon," his dad said.

"What is it?"

"A Mule."

"A mule? What are we going to do with a mule?"

"I just thought it would be nice to have a Mule. I'm thinking of getting some chickens too."

Paul shrugged. His dad was getting a little strange in the head.

The boys went outside with Patrick and played in the grass until dark. The little dog was worn out from playing ball and rope pull. They said goodnight to the parents and went to their room. Paul went in the bathroom first and washed up and brushed his teeth and then Anton took his turn.

"This was the best day ever," Anton said as he slipped into his bed.

"It was good wasn't it?"

"I'll never forget you for this," he said to Paul.

"Hey, it's all good for me too. I have a new brother and he's got a dog I can play with too."

"Patrick is half yours, you know."

"I think he's pretty tired out."

They looked down on the floor and the little dog was lying

in his bed on his back sleeping like a little angel.

"A tired boy," Anton whispered.

"Good night," Paul said.

"Good night Paul."

Paul lay there thinking about the day. It had been great. How his life had changed by meeting a silent boy. He heard some commotion and looked at Anton's bed. Patrick was on his hind feet trying to jump up on the bed next to Anton. The boy looked down and grinned and lifted him up. The dog snuggled down next to him and closed his eyes.

Anton looked across the room and smiled.

Chapter 20

P aul woke and stretched. He sat on the edge of his bed and looked across the room. Anton and Patrick were lying next to each other. The little dog was snuggled with his back against Anton's chest and he had his arm across him. They looked pretty content.

Paul picked up his shorts and tee shirt and quietly slipped into the bathroom. When he finished he walked to the kitchen barefoot. His mom was making breakfast.

"Where's Anton?"

"He and Patrick were still sleeping," Paul said.

"Is the dog in his bed?"

Paul nodded.

"I knew he'd end up there. Well I guess it's not so bad."

"He started out in his own bed but soon he snuck up there."

Paul's dad came into the kitchen.

"So how did the first night go with the pup?"

"The two of them are snuggled together in Anton's bed," Paul said smiling.

"He sure loves that little dog," his dad said.

"He's made a big change in just a few days."

Just then Anton came hustling past the kitchen in his boxers carrying Patrick in his arms.

"Patrick's gotta pee," he said hurriedly.

The two of them disappeared out the front door and the family looked out to see Anton standing there in his underwear while the little dog squatted to pee. Then he sniffed around for a while and hunched up and pooped. Anton called him and they came back inside.

"He was a good boy! He made a pee and a poop."

Paul's folks were smiling widely.

"How about some breakfast Sweetie?"

"Yeah, I'm hungry."

Then he looked down and realized he was in his underwear. He turned red.

"Oh sorry, I forgot to get dressed. I was in a pretty big hurry."

"Don't worry, we're all family here," Paul's dad said.

Anton smiled and sprinted to the bedroom with Patrick following him. I few minutes later he came back with his tee shirt and shorts on and his face still partly wet from washing.

They all sat and ate their breakfast. Patrick sat beside his master and looked up at the table.

"I think Patrick is hungry too," Paul said.

"See if he'd like a little piece of bacon," Nancy said.

Anton broke a little piece off and held it down for the dog. He sniffed it and gobbled it down.

"He likes it," Anton said.

"Who doesn't like bacon," Paul said.

After breakfast the boys helped clean up the dishes while Paul's parents got ready for work.

"What should I call them?" Anton asked.

"Who Mom and Dad?"

He nodded.

"Well it depends on how you feel about living here. I'm happy to call you my brother. If you feel okay about it why not call them Mom and Dad too?"

"Ya think they'd mind?"

"Try them."

They finished the dishes and walked out onto the porch. It was going to be a beautiful day.

74

"We should go up and look at the dam and see what we need to fix it," Paul said.

"Yeah, that'd be great," Anton said.

Just then the parents came out.

"Dad, Mom, Anton would like to call you Dad and Mom, is that okay with you?"

The parents looked at Anton and both smiled.

"We'd love that Sweetie. If you feel comfortable about calling us that, then we'd love it," Nancy said.

"I mean, I know this is just temporary, this Foster Home thing, but I really like it here and I…"

"It's only temporary unless we make it permanent… if you want it to be permanent," Paul's dad said.

"It's up to me?"

They nodded. "If you want to stay here, we'd love to have you stay here permanently."

Anton's eyes filled with tears.

"It would be good to have a family again," he said.

They all hugged and all had a few tears. Patrick jumped up on Anton's legs trying to get some attention.

"Okay, so that's it. You call us Mom and Dad," Paul's dad said.

Anton nodded.

"Okay Mom and Dad, we'll see you later," he said smiling widely.

The parents left for work in their vehicles and the boys stood there watching them drive off.

"Well brother, let's take a walk up to the pond," Paul said.

They put on their flip-flops and set out up the valley with Patrick galloping along behind them sniffing all the new wonderful smells and taking in all the new sights.

Chapter 21

When they got to what was left of the old pond they looked it over to see what they needed to do to fix it. Many of the stones had washed down the creek, probably during high rains and most of the timbers were gone also. Many of the largest stones were there and in the creek below the old dam so they could re-use them. There were hundreds of downed trees up on the hill where the tornado had gone through so they could get timbers there.

"There's a place up on the hill where the rocks have all slid down the side of the hill. That's where we got the stones."

"We can use some of these stones and there are some down the creek that we can salvage too," Paul said. "All we have to do is wade around and find them."

Anton nodded.

"Then if Dad gets us a 4-wheeler we can start hauling new stones."

Paul looked across the valley where the tornado went up over the ridge.

"We can take a chain saw up there and cut some timbers for the dam too," he said, pointing at the trees. "We can make firewood up there too. We'll have enough firewood for years with all those trees on the ground."

"There's a cave up by the rockslide too," Anton said.

"A cave? Wow, let's walk up there."

Paul followed Anton up the hillside. Patrick scampered ahead of them happily checking out all the wonderful new things he found.

When they got to the base of the hill Anton stopped and looked up at the rocks. He looked from side to side until he figured out where he was exactly. Then he started climbing up through the rocks and Paul followed him.

"It's up here... I think. Things have changed a little since I was up here the last time."

When they got part way up the hill Anton stopped and picked up a stick and began poking at the mud bank.

"When it rains really hard a lot of mud slides down and fills the entrance," he said.

Finally the stick went into the ground real easy. He poked around a bit and a big chunk of mud fell into the hill. They knelt down and dug with their hands. Soon Patrick was between them digging with his little paws. Anton beamed when he saw the dog helping them.

They cleared out an opening and looked inside. Indeed it was a cave.

"Old Patrick and I went inside. A little way in there's a place where some rocks block the opening but Patrick went through and was gone for a long time. I think it goes in there a long way."

"Another thing for us to check out this summer," Paul said.

Just then they heard the sound of a big horn from a truck like a semi. They looked down the valley and a semi with a flatbed on behind it pulled up in front of the house. On the back of the flatbed was a green vehicle that looked like a cross between a small truck and a 4-wheeler.

"That must be the Mule Dad told us was coming."

"I thought he meant a mule, like Hee-Haw," Anton said.

"I think he meant this thing. Let's go."

They hustled down to the house and the guy driving the truck was taking the chains off the vehicle.

"Are you the guys who are waiting for this?"

"I guess so, we expected a mule, like an animal. I guess our dad was playing a joke on us."

"This is a cool little truck. It's 4-wheel drive, has plenty of power, can carry stuff on the back and can drive nearly anywhere."

Paul and Anton were beaming. This is just what they needed for the dam project.

The man put some tracks down and then drove the vehicle off onto the driveway. He showed them how everything worked and handed them the keys.

"Have fun boys," he said as he got in his truck and drove off.

They stood there looking at the thing. It was really cool. It was dark green, had a nice padded bench seat in front, an overhead roof over the driver's compartment, and a steel box like a truck box on the back.

"What do you think?"

"I think it's perfect," Anton said.

"We should try it out."

Anton grinned. "Really?"

"We might as well see how it works."

They checked the gas tank and it was full. They got in and Paul drove. Patrick sat on Anton's lap and his tail wagged like mad.

They took off slowly and soon got the feel for the thing. In no time they were zooming up the valley, wind streaming through their hair, laughing their heads off.

"Oh this is going to be fun," Paul said.

"Just like Christmas AND a bag of chips."

Chapter 22

They drove up by the pond and parked the Mule and got out. Patrick scampered down by the water and peed.

"He still pees like a girl," Anton said.

"Give him time."

They walked down by the dam. It was obvious that there had been some big rainstorms over the past two years that had caused the dam to wash out. Many of the rocks were scattered downstream from it.

"We need some larger rocks this time," Anton said.

"With two of us, we should be able to get bigger rocks and more of them," Paul replied.

"It will be better if we use some of the trees that blew down too. Last time I used planks and branches," Anton said.

"Let's go get a load of rocks," Paul suggested.

They walked to the Mule and Paul told Anton to drive. He grinned from ear to ear as he got in the driver's seat. Paul called Patrick and he jumped up on the floorboard where Paul picked him up and held him in his lap. Anton started the vehicle up and they drove up the valley to the rockslide.

Anton backed the Mule up as far as he could get it to the pile of rocks and they parked and got out. Patrick took off immediately exploring and the two boys climbed up to the rocks and began choosing some to haul back. They rolled some of the rocks down by the Mule and slid some that wouldn't roll. In half an hour they had plenty of them by the Mule so they loaded up several.

"Let's go with these," Paul said. "We don't want to overload it and bust something."

The called Patrick and carefully drove back down the hill and to the pond. Anton backed up as close to the dam as he could get and then they unloaded the rocks onto the existing ones leftover from the first dam.

"Well that's a start," Paul said looking at the small improvement.

"It's gonna take a lot of rocks," Anton said. "Last time it took me a few weeks to build it."

"With two of us it won't take so long," Paul said.

"I'm hungry," Anton said rubbing his belly.

Paul checked his phone and it was nearly noon.

"Time to eat," he said.

They drove back to the house. Paul looked in the refrigerator and found a package of wieners. They took the wieners and a package of buns, a bag of chips and a bag of cookies to the patio. Paul fired up the grill and they cooked the wieners over the fire. Then they sat at the table and ate.

"This is a really cool place," Anton said.

He looked around the patio. It was like an outdoor kitchen. He looked at the hot tub.

"Have you ever used that?"

"Yeah I have a few times."

"I've never been in one of those."

"Let's try it."

"Really?"

"Sure, we've got plenty of time. Unless you want to go haul more rocks."

"Let's take a break."

They went to their bedroom and put on their swimming suits. Then they turned on the water jets and heater and sat on the edge of the tub and waited while the water warmed up.

"It feels pretty warm," Paul said and he slipped into the water. Anton slid in after him. They both leaned back against the side and let the jets of water shoot over them.

"Wow this feels nice," Anton said.

Suddenly there was a small splash and Patrick popped up from under the water. He'd jumped in off the deck that surrounded the tub. The little dog began dogpaddling around and Anton laughed and grabbed him.

He held the dog against his chest and Patrick licked his face.

They sat for a while and just talked about themselves and their past. They really knew very little about each other.

Paul told him about all the places they'd lived while his dad was in the military.

After a while Paul asked Anton if he knew where the water from the stream started.

"I know it's up in the hills someplace but I never went up there. There has to be a spring somewhere. That's why it's so cold."

"We should go and look."

"Yeah that sounds fun."

They shut the tub down and got out. Patrick shook off and the boys toweled off and then changed back into shorts and tee shirts. Paul drove and they went up the valley, past the pond and followed the stream up to the end of the valley.

About a quarter of a mile from the pond the stream turned and headed up between two very steep hills. It was rocky and brushy so they parked the Mule and walked along the stream and followed it where it went up into the woods at the floor of the valley.

"It goes up a long way," Paul said looking through the trees.

"Have you ever been up there?"

"I had a trail up here."

"What kind of trail?"

"I had a Kawasaki dirt bike. I made trails all over the farm and up on the next farm too. When I lived here before, that farm was abandoned. I've got trails all over the place."

"Cool, so what happened to your bike?"

Anton shrugged. "The last time I saw it, it was going up into the air."

"Wow, I wonder where it landed?"

"I don't know. It might be up on the other farm, or it might be in the next county."

Paul shrugged. "Let's see."

They hiked along. It was brushy and steep but they took their time. The stream became smaller and smaller as they hiked up the ditch between the two hills.

Anton noticed Patrick ahead of them and he seemed like he was stopped. Then he saw a fence across the valley and down into the ditch.

"There's a fence," he said.

"That wasn't here before," Anton said.

They walked up to the fence and were surprised. It looked pretty new. It was six feet tall made of woven wire. On top of the woven wire was a strand of barbed wire.

A little way down the line was a sign on the fence and they walked to it.

NO TRESPASSING
PRIVATE PROPERTY

Below the letters there was a picture of a smoking gun.

"Wow they don't mince words do they?"

"They sure don't want anyone on their land."

"Well then we better not look any farther," Paul said.

They walked back down to the Mule. As they were driving back to the house Paul looked over at Anton.

"So you don't know if that was there before?"

"It wasn't there. I went up that valley on one side and came back down on the other. There were some old fences that were falling down but nothing like that one."

"I wonder what's going on up there that they are so worried about someone seeing them?"

"Hunters?"

"I've never heard of hunters threatening to shoot someone."

"Strange,"

Chapter 23

"Dad do you know who owns the land north of us?" Paul asked at the patio picnic table that evening.

"No I don't, why?"

"Anton and I went up to the end of the valley and followed the stream today. We just thought it would be cool to see where it started. When we got up the valley where the stream comes from we came to a high fence topped with barbed wire and a sign telling us to keep out. There was a picture of a gun on the sign."

"Hmm, not very friendly are they?"

"No we didn't go past the fence but it seems strange that they'd be so nasty about it."

"I'll check with the county tomorrow. They have property records."

"So how is your dam going?" Nancy asked.

"We started today on it. The Mule is going to work really well. That thing climbs up those hills like crazy. We do need to use the chainsaw eventually though," Paul said.

"Oh are you sure you want to do that?" his mom asked.

"We need some timbers in the dam," Anton said.

"You've used it before haven't you?" his dad asked.

"Yeah lots of times. We'll be careful, I promise."

They ate dinner out in the yard and had a nice evening. After dinner the boys went to their room and played Playstation while the parents watched TV.

"So what's the plan tomorrow?" Anton asked.

"You're the dam builder. I'll follow your directions."

Anton grinned.

"We need a few more rows of rocks and then some timers. Then we'll alternate and it will be really solid. Last time I used sod to fill the holes. We need to find something to use for that too."

"Sounds good. I'm ready for bed. I want to get an early start tomorrow."

They used the bathroom and soon they were both sleeping and Patrick was snuggled next to Anton.

The next day they hauled two rows of rocks and decided it was time to add some timber. The pile was getting shaky and they didn't want it to fall over. They went back to the house and got the chainsaw and drove up the valley to the swath of downed trees.

Anton got out of the Mule and stood there looking up at all the destruction. He seemed a little shaken now that he was so close to it.

"Are you okay?"

He nodded.

"I was just thinking of that night. It was dark but there was a lot of lightning. It all happened so fast but I remember seeing trees just like they were lying down in front of me. There was stuff in the air hitting me and flying past.

Paul put his arm around the boy's shoulder.

"It must have been terrifying."

Anton nodded.

"I thought I was going to die."

"But you made it."

He nodded. "But I lost Patrick."

His eyes filled with tears and he turned away. Paul left him alone.

"I landed down there in the swamp," he said.

"That was what saved you I heard."

"They said because I landed in that soft ground I didn't die. It sure as heck didn't feel soft when I hit it."

"Well if I ever go to Las Vegas gambling, I want you to go with me," Paul said.

Anton grinned.

"Okay that's a deal."

They got the chainsaw out and began cutting trees they knew they could lift onto the Mule. They measured them and cut them into the correct length. They planned on dropping them to the sides of the piles of rock to keep the rocks stable and to keep them from washing away in high water.

They piled six logs on the back of the Mule and strapped them down. Then they drove slowly back down the hill to the creek.

"One of us needs to be on the other side," Anton said.

"I'll go," Paul volunteered.

He took off his shoes and shirt and then decided to take off his shorts. He waded into the creek and across to the other side. Anton lifted one of the timbers up and let it fall across the pile of rocks. Paul took one end and Anton took the other and they maneuvered it into place. They did the same with the other five and then Paul waded back across.

"Boy that looks good," Anton said as Paul stripped off his wet boxers and put his shorts on.

"That really stiffened it up," Paul said.

"Next time one of us can walk across on the dam and not have to get wet," Anton said smiling.

"What do you think? Enough work for one day?"

Anton nodded.

"How about a hot tub."

"Okey dokey."

Chapter 24

The next morning the boys got up and ate breakfast and hurried up to the pond to see how high the water had risen. They drove up to the bank and were pretty disappointed.

"It hardly came up at all," Paul said looking at the nearly empty pond.

"Last time it filled up over night," Anton said.

"What's different?"

They got off the Mule and walked down by the dam. There was a lot of water trickling through the rocks and logs. Paul looked up at the creek above the pond and the stream was much lower than it usually was.

"The creek isn't running as fast and with it running so slow the water is going out as fast as it comes in," he said.

"I don't know why the creek is running so slowly, but last time I packed sod chunks in between the rocks. That is the only thing different than before," Anton said.

They took off their shoes and waded down into the creek. It was obvious that the cracks between the rocks were too large to hold water.

"Where did you get the sod?"

"I got it up there where the rocks are. The whole hillside caved away after a big rain and there were big thick chunks of sod with lots of roots. I hauled them down here and packed them into the cracks. Then once there were sticks and logs on them the natural leaves and stuff that came down the creek kept the cracks filled. The dam leaked a little but not like this."

"We need some sod."

"It's all gone. I used it all up and what is left is just a pile of dirt now."

"Hmm, that's not good. We need to find something to replace the sod."

"What can we use?" Anton asked.

"I'm not sure. But I think we should run into town to the garden center and see if they have any suggestions. They build ponds and water features for people. I bet they have something we can use."

"Cool idea," Anton said.

They called Patrick and he came up out of the weeds carrying a turtle in his mouth. Anton took it away from him and put it in the creek.

"Good boy Patrick."

They decided to drive the Mule to the garden center. It was fun to drive and if they found something they could haul it in the back. They drove down to the end of the lane and Paul stopped to check for traffic on the road. Luckily he stopped fully because a beat-up pickup truck came flying past and nearly hit them. The old pickup was a faded blue with a red door on the passenger side.

"What the?"

"Jeez, those guys were driving like crazy," Anton said.

"I wonder where they came from? I've never seen that old truck around here before."

"Who lives up that road?"

"I didn't think anyone lived up there," Paul said. "The road goes up to an old farm that's pretty much worthless. The few buildings that are there are just junk and there's not much land for planting stuff. We looked at it when we were looking for a place to build a house but it was so far up in the boondocks Mom didn't want to live there."

"Well maybe they're campers or something."

"I don't know but we're lucky we didn't pull out or we'd be toast."

They drove on to town and to the garden center. When they got there the old blue pickup was parked in the parking lot.

"There's that truck," Paul said.

"Did you see who was driving it?"

"Nope, I was too busy keeping from getting wrecked."

Anton put Patrick on the seat of the Mule and told him to stay. The dog sat down and wagged his tail.

"You think he'll stay there?" Paul asked.

"I've been working with him on commands. He gets it right most of the time. I guess we'll see."

They went into the place. They looked around for a bit and then asked a sales clerk about the pond sealer. She directed them to a guy in the ponds department.

Paul explained what they were doing and the guy listened and then had them follow him.

"What you need is a pond liner. We use them to build ponds and water features. They're real thick rubber liners. You can put one on the upstream side of the dam and it will hold the water for you."

That was just what they needed. They looked at the liners and found one that was about the size of the dam when it would be finished. Paul had them put it on his parent's charge account.

While he was at the cash register Anton walked to a display of patio stones. He was looking at them when Paul walked up carrying the liner.

"What'cha looking at?"

"I was thinking it would be nice to get a flat rock like this for Patrick's grave," he said quietly.

Paul looked at the stone display. There were many shapes and sizes and colors. Some had engraving on them.

"Pick one we'll get it."

"Are you sure?"

"Hey don't worry about it."

Anton picked a light tan stone and they took it to the

counter.

"Do you want it engraved?" the girl asked."

"We can get that done here?"

"We have a machine. You can do it but it's a hard job and doesn't usually turn out as well as you'd like. It only costs fifty cents per letter."

Paul looked at Anton and he nodded.

"We'd like Patrick engraved on it," Anton said.

The girl called a clerk on the PA system and a guy came and said he'd be back in five minutes. They looked around and Anton poked Paul in the ribs.

"Look there," he said nodding to the parking lot.

There were two dark skinned guys getting into the blue pickup. They were short, dark and kind of dangerous looking. They started up the truck and backed out without looking behind them. Then they sped out of the parking lot.

"Nice guys," Anton said.

"I wonder what those guys are doing up there?"

"They don't look like campers," Anton said.

"They sure don't."

Just then the clerk came back with the stone. It looked very nice. Paul walked over and picked up a pot with a geranium in it and they paid for the two items and the engraving. Anton looked happy as they got in the Mule. New Patrick was very interested in the flower.

Anton hugged the little guy.

"Well, back to the pond," Paul said.

Chapter 25

O n the way back out of town they stopped at KFC and got some chicken and sides. They ate in the Mule so Patrick could have his share too.

"I wonder what those Mexican guys are doing up on that old farm?" Paul said.

"How do you know they're Mexicans?"

"Well they look like Mexicans. They're short and dark skinned and have black hair. I don't think they're Norwegians."

Anton laughed.

"I guess that's a pretty good guess. I hope they were just passing by. They acted kind of hard. I don't think they'd be real friendly neighbors."

They got back to the valley and drove up to the pond. It was a bit fuller than it had been.

"Look, the stream is running faster now. I wonder what made it run so slow earlier?" Paul said.

"I have no idea. When I lived here before, it ran full all the time. I never saw it go slower, even in the middle of the summer when it was really dry."

"Hmm, it's a mystery for sure," Paul said.

They got out and Anton carried the stone over to Old Patrick's grave. He pulled the wooden cross out of the ground and took a shovel and dug a little slot in the ground. Then he stood the stone up in the slot and filled in back and front of it so it stood up on it's own. Then Paul helped him dig another hole and they planted the geranium. Paul ran down to the pond and got a pail of water and they watered the plant.

Paul stood up and looked it over.

"It looks real nice," he said.

Anton nodded. He didn't look up and Paul knew he was probably weeping so he said he'd go unload the pond liner.

Anton knelt on the ground next to the dog's grave. He patted the earth over his friend's resting place.

"I'm sorry I didn't take better care of you Patrick. I did my best but it wasn't good enough. I miss you. I'll come and see you every day."

He wiped the tears from his eyes and walked down to the pond. Paul was standing there looking at the dam.

"You know what we have to do," he said.

"We have to take the timbers off and put the liner down first," Anton said.

"Yup, that's the only way to fix it right."

"That means we have to get in the water and do it," Anton said.

"Yup. Let's run down to the house and change into some old shorts and some old tennis shoes. I have a some that are wrecked. They'll be good for working on this."

They drove the Mule down and changed and grabbed a heavy-duty scissors. When they got back they went down to the dam and Paul waded across to the other side. One by one they moved the logs off the dam so only the rocks were left behind. Then they unfolded the rubber liner and laid it on the rocks on the upstream side of the dam. It was too large so they trimmed it. Then they took the biggest log and maneuvered it down into the water and wedged it against the rocks, holding the rubber liner in place. One by one they added the logs back to the upper side until they had the thing all re-built. There was a lot of extra rubber left on top and they folded it up and left it so they could un-fold it when they added the next layer of rocks and logs.

They waded out of the water and sat on the grass.

"Wow my feet are frozen," Anton said pulling off the wet shoes.

"That water is cold. You said you used to swim in it?"

"When the pond was full it warmed up because the sun shined on it. I think if we ever get it full we'll be able to swim."

They inspected the lower side of the dam and were very pleased. There was just a trickle of water seeping through. The pond was filling too.

"That's going to do it," Paul said.

"Yup, this will work even better than the sod."

They stood admiring their work and Patrick came out of the tall grass all covered with mud, carrying a frog in his mouth.

"Here comes our retriever," Paul said laughing.

Anton took the frog from the dog's mouth. It was a little muddy but seemed to be okay so he let it go into the water. Patrick looked at him strangely.

"Looks like he's mad you let his treasure go," Paul said.

"That was a good boy," he said to the dog. Patrick wagged his tail excitedly.

"Well I've had enough pond work for one day," Paul said.

"How about a hot tub?"

They both thought that was a good idea. After wading in the cold water for a couple of hours a nice soak would feel good. They drove home and washed up first and then got in the hot tub.

"I keep thinking about those guys in the truck," Paul said.

"Did you see what they got at the garden center?" Anton asked.

"No I didn't pay any attention."

"I saw one of them carrying bags of what looked like fertilizer and putting them in the truck."

"Fertilizer? I wonder what they're growing up there?"

"Well it must be a bunch of something. I saw him carry at least ten big bags of the stuff."

Paul looked curiously at Anton.

"I'm gonna call down there."

He got out of the hot tub and dried off. Then he got his phone and the phone book and called the garden center.

"Hi I was in there earlier and got a rubber liner for a pond. Yeah, it worked just perfect. Huh? Oh no problems at all. I was just wondering who waited on those two Mexican guys with the blue pickup. Sure I'll wait."

"Do they know who did?" Anton asked.

"I don't know. I'm waiting. Oh yeah, this is Paul Daniels. I was wondering what you know about those two Mexican guys in the blue pickup. Have they been around here long?"

He listened for a while and then thanked the guy and hung up.

"What?" Anton asked.

"He said they've been here a few weeks. They bought a bunch of plastic hose and a water pump. This week they've been back twice and bought fertilizer."

"Hmm, they're growing something."

"Yeah, no doubt. The guy at the garden center said they always pay for everything in cash too. Usually twenty dollar bills."

"Hmm, that's kind of unusual."

"No kidding."

Chapter 26

"**D**ad did you find out who owns the land up the valley from us?" Paul asked at dinner.

"It was some corporation," his dad said. "I don't remember the exact name. Why do you ask?"

Paul explained the strange guys who they ran into at the garden center.

"I'll call the realtor tomorrow and ask," his dad said. "You guys stay away from that place. If they have a picture of a gun on their signs you don't need to go near the place."

"We weren't planning on it. We were just curious."

The boys drove up to the pond and then went up to the rockslide and loaded up a load of rocks. They built up another row on the dam and then did the same thing again. Then they went up to the hillside and cut some timbers and hauled them down. The water was about half way up the side of their dam. The pond was filling.

"Let's get the rubber liner up on the side and then fit the logs on it," Paul said.

They were both wearing old cutoffs and they waded into the water and built up the side and then anchored the liner with the logs. The water now had about two and a half feet to go up the side.

"How high should we make it?" Paul asked.

"This is about as high as I had it last time."

"I think one more row of rocks and timbers and then we'll

bring a couple of bigger timbers down and make a wider top so we can walk back and forth across it," Paul suggested.

Anton thought that was a swell idea.

They went to the house and had some sandwiches and then went up and hauled enough rocks to finish the dam. When they had them all placed Anton looked around for Patrick. The dog was laying on the grave of Old Patrick.

"Look at that," he said.

"Isn't that something? It's like he knows the old dog is there."

"He's growing isn't he?" Anton said.

"Yeah, we see him every day but he's grown a lot since you got him."

"He's sure a good boy," Anton said smiling.

Paul just grinned at his friend. What a change he'd made.

"Well do you have enough energy for a couple more logs?"

"Yeah, let's go," Anton said, calling Patrick.

They drove up and cut two logs for the side of the dam and then two longer ones for the top. The logs were getting longer and heavier as they went up on the dam. The last two for the top were pretty good-sized ones and they had a hard time getting them down the side of the bank.

Then Paul got in the water and they floated one and then the other across and lifted and dragged them up on top of the dam.

"Wait a second," Paul said just before they got the last log in place.

He went to the middle of the dam and removed two rocks, leaving a low spot.

"This way water can run through here when the pond gets full. If we leave it closed the water will go up and around the end. If we get a big rain it might wash out the earth on the ends and there goes our dam.

Anton stood there looking at his friend.

"You're a lot smarter than you look," he said.

"Um... thanks," Paul said.

Then Anton broke out laughing.

"You little turd," Paul said grinning.

They got the two top logs in place on top of the dam. Paul was on the other side so he decided to test it. He stepped out onto the logs and started across. The logs wiggled a bit but held pretty solidly.

"You know what we should do?" he said stepping off the other side.

"What?"

"We should get some short boards and nail them on top of the logs to make a better place to walk and to tie the whole thing together. We could do it first thing tomorrow."

"Does that mean a trip to town?"

Paul nodded.

"Can we stop at KFC?"

"We'd be fools not to,"

Chapter 27

"**I** found out who owns that land north of us," Paul's dad said at dinner.

"Really?"

"Well it's public records so I just called the County Clerk of Records. I really didn't find out much. The recorded landowner is Buena Vista properties. They have a mailing address in Milwaukee. So that tells us almost nothing."

"Hmm, they must be growing something up there. They bought a bunch of fertilizer," Anton said.

"If I remember right, we looked at that place and it was mostly woods and a small open area at the bottom of the valley. There wouldn't be much area to plant corn or anything like that."

"Well, it's not important. We just were surprised to see guys like that around here. They're sure not locals."

"Well just stay away from them," his mom said.

"We will, do you need anything from town? We're going in tomorrow for some slats to nail across our bridge over the dam."

"Now it's a bridge too?"

Paul grinned. "We got a little carried away. But it's really nice. Our pond should be filled in a day or two."

"Um I was thinking," Anton said, "When I built my dam my dad..." he stopped for a second, "My dad had a load of sand brought up there so we had a beach. Some of it is still there but it would be nice if we had some more to fix it up."

"I think that can be arranged. I'll call for some in the

morning. Put some stakes out where you want it dropped."

The boys said they would do just that.

"Thanks," Anton said, "Dad."

Chuck smiled and ruffled Anton's hair.

"No problem Son."

"You're parents are really nice people," Anton said later as they lay in their beds.

"Our parents," Paul corrected.

"Yeah, I forgot. I still feel a little strange calling them Mom and Dad."

"Well don't. As far as they're concerned you and Patrick are family."

Anton looked down at the dog lying on his back. His ears were splayed out from his head and he was snoring loudly.

"How can such a little dog make so much noise?" he asked grinning.

"As long as it comes out of that end and not the other I'm all for it."

"That's true. Well goodnight Brother."

"Goodnight Brother."

They took four sticks with orange ribbons on them and drove them into the ground where they wanted the sand dumped just in case they didn't get back from town before the sand got there.

When they got to the end of the lane Paul stopped and looked to the left.

"Let's take a drive up that way and see if we can see anything."

"What if we get shot?"

"Well, that won't be good. But I doubt they'd shoot at us on a public road."

They drove about a mile up the road and came to the lane

that ran into the other property. There was a steel gate at the lane and it was locked. There was one of the signs with the picture of the gun on it attached to the gate.

"Real friendly," Anton said.

"No kidding," Paul said. He put the vehicle in reverse and backed around into the road. Just as he did that the blue pickup came rumbling down the lane. There were two Mexican-looking guys in it. One was the driver from the other day and the other was a different guy.

"Morning," Paul said trying to be friendly.

The passenger got out and scowled at them. He took a key and opened the gate. The driver drove through and the other guy locked it up again. Then they sat there looking at the boys.

"I guess they want us to go first," Anton said quietly.

"It seems so."

Paul put the vehicle into drive and they pulled away.

"Have a nice day," Anton said as they went past.

"Oh sure. Now they'll probably start shooting," Paul said.

"I'm getting on the floor. Come here Patrick, let's get down."

Anton knelt on the floor and laughed as Paul drove on unprotected. He looked over his shoulder and the truck was right behind them. He turned into their lane and it went past.

Once they were down the road a little way the boys pulled out behind them.

"Two can play that 'follow' game."

It soon became clear they were going to the garden center just like Paul and Anton were. The blue truck was parked and they parked a little way away from it.

"Let's see what they buy today," Anton said quietly.

"Don't make them mad. They probably have a cannon in the truck."

Paul found the lumber area and got some treated 1 x 6s for the top of the dam. Anton snuck around until he saw the guys loading up some irrigation pipes. He watched them as they carried the stuff to the truck. Then one of them walked over to the Mule and looked inside. Patrick came up from the floor barking at the guy. He backed off and made a move to slap the dog.

"Don't even think about it!" Paul said coming from behind the guy.

"Try bite me!"

"He wouldn't bite you if you weren't nosing around our vehicle."

"Why you follow?"

"We didn't follow you. We came here for lumber."

Paul motioned to the pile of boards on a cart from the lumber area of the place.

"You snoop."

"It's a free country pal. We have as much right on that highway as you do. You don't like it, call the police."

"No policea!"

"That's up to you. Stay away from our vehicle and we'll stay away from you."

The guy muttered something in Spanish and walked off.

By now Anton had arrived.

"Did he hit Patrick?"

"No he acted like he was going to but he didn't."

"He better not."

Paul grinned. "You think you could take him?"

Anton grinned back. "If I got mad enough and had one of those boards."

"Let's go to KFC."

Chapter 28

They went through the drive-through at KFC and ate in the Mule so Patrick could have something to eat too. The little dog was growing daily and had an appetite like a horse.

"Patrick's getting big," Paul said.

"He's almost full grown already," Anton said proudly looking at the dog. "He looks just like Old Patrick."

"I think that's a common trait in beagles," Paul said grinning.

Anton smiled. "You know what I mean."

They finished and drove home. They went to the garage and set up Paul's dad's miter saw and cut a whole bunch of the boards to a length of two feet. Then they took a sack of nails and a couple of hammers and headed for the pond.

The truck had delivered the load of sand so they smoothed it out and pulled the tall grass that grew near the edge of the pond in front of their beach.

Then they decided to finish their bridge, so they laid one of the boards across the two logs and Paul nailed it down. Then they laid another next to it, leaving an inch space, and nailed it down too. It was going to take a long time to get them all nailed down.

"I'm going to take some across and start from the other side," Paul said. "You keep working here."

Paul picked up a stack of the boards and stuck a bunch of

nails in his pocket, grabbed his hammer and tightrope-walked across the bridge. When he got to the other side he began nailing boards down and working toward the middle. Anton worked on the other side and after half an hour they were just about to the middle. Luckily they could space the boards so they met pretty evenly in the middle. Paul nailed the last one in place. They both stood up and surveyed their bridge.

"Looks pretty good," Anton said.

"This should last for a long time," Paul added.

"You know, as much as I hate to make more work for us, I think we should cut two or three more logs and wedge them against the lower side of the dam to keep it upright in case there would be a big rain and flood. I'd sure hate to see the whole thing topple over into the creek," Paul said.

"I thought of that too but kind of hated to say anything," Anton said grinning.

"We might as well do it right."

They went back and got the chainsaw and drove up to the hillside and cut three braces. Then they carried them down and wedged them against the lower side of the dam.

"That's not going anywhere now," Anton said.

They stood there and looked over their handiwork. It was a fine dam.

"Well, I think now that everything is ready, we should set up our tent and sleep up here tonight," Anton said.

"Good idea."

They walked to the Mule and called Patrick. He was nowhere to be found.

"I wonder where he went?" Anton said looking worried.

"He wouldn't have gone far. You know beagles. They wander... looking for stuff and suddenly they find that they've wandered away. He'll show up."

They called and called and soon Patrick came trotting down from the hill. He was carrying a glove.

"Where did you get that?" Paul asked taking it from the dog.

"It's a work glove. You don't suppose he went under that fence and found it up in the valley?"

"Patrick, no!" Anton said.

"No," he said pointing to the glove.

The dog looked chastised and lowered his head.

"Oh boy now you hurt his feelings," Paul said.

"Better his feelings than him getting shot," Anton replied.

They loaded up in the Mule and drove to the house. They piled all of the camping gear into the back of the Mule and hauled it up to the pond. Then they set up the tent and got their campsite organized.

"We need a fire ring," Paul said.

"Some rocks," Anton nodded.

So they drove up to the rockslide and piled some rocks for a fire pit in the back. Paul looked up at the cave opening.

"While we're here, let's go up and take a look in there," he said.

Anton looked over the seat. "There is a shovel back there. Do we have a light?"

Paul reached under his seat and pulled out a flashlight.

"Let's go."

It hadn't rained since they'd first opened the cave so the opening was easy to find. They climbed up to it. It looked like a triangle with the point at the top. They dug mud and rocks away and the bottom got wider as they removed more and more debris. Anton crawled inside and shoveled more dirt out once it was open far enough.

Paul crawled inside and Patrick followed, his nose sniffing and his tail wagging.

"This is pretty cool," Paul said looking over the small room.

"Up ahead there's another triangle opening like at the front. I think if we dig there we can get through that next opening too.

I don't know what's past it."

"That's where Old Patrick went?"

Anton nodded. "He crawled in there and was gone for a long time. I don't know how far away he was but he was gone long enough that I was pretty worried."

"Well, let's dig."

They dug dirt away from the opening but as they dug the dirt clogged up the place they were working. They needed to get rid of the dirt they were digging.

"I'll run down to the pond and get a plastic bucket," Paul said. "Then we can fill it and dump the dirt so we have more room to work."

Anton kept digging as Paul got the bucket. Soon he was back and they cleaned up all of the dirt on the cave floor and then shoveled the new dirt right into the bucket. When it was full one of them would drag it to the opening and dump it down the hill.

They worked for over an hour and finally had an opening that was large enough for them to crawl through.

"Well?" Paul said.

"I'll go first," Anton replied.

He turned to crawl through and saw Patrick's tail disappearing into the hole.

"Patrick! Come back here!"

The dog was gone.

Chapter 29

A nton got down on his belly and shinnied through the hole. It was very dark on the other side and he had to wait for Paul to come through with the flashlight.

"Patrick!"

They waited. The dog didn't appear.

"We have to go in there and find him," Anton said urgently.

"Didn't Old Patrick do this too?"

"Yes he did."

"He came back."

"I know but he was a lot older. He knew better than to go too far. I can't wait. Give me the flashlight and I'll go alone."

"No we'll go together," Paul said. "Here take the light and you go ahead. I'll be right behind you."

The tunnel was about four feet tall and about the same width. They had to hunch over and walk with their knees bent to keep from hitting their heads on the top. The tunnel snaked around back and forth for a long way. After probably a hundred feet the tunnel split into two new tunnels.

They sat on the floor and looked down each one.

"Which do you think?" Anton asked.

"Shine the light on the floor."

They looked for footprints. The floor was mostly just rock but there was a little dry mud in places. Anton moved forward in the left tunnel for a little way and then came back and tried the right one.

"Here's a track," he said.

They followed the right tunnel. The opening got a bit smaller and seemed to be going uphill. It wasn't long and they came to a steep rise in the floor that went even more uphill.

"It's heading up. It probably comes out on the top of the hill," Paul said.

"There wouldn't be snakes or animals in here would there be?"

"It's pretty cool in here for a snake. I don't know what other animals would be in here for. There isn't anything for them to eat. Unless they were hiding there'd be no reason for them to be here."

"Patrick!" Anton yelled. The sound echoed down the passageways.

"Let's keep going," Paul said.

Now it was very obvious that they were going uphill. The tunnel split again a short way ahead. They again looked for tracks. Anton found one little partial paw print in some mud and they again took the right side of the split. This tunnel was even smaller, making them crawl on their hands and knees.

"How far do you think we've come?" Anton asked.

"It seems like miles but it's probably a couple of hundred feet, maybe three hundred."

"Like a football field?"

"Yeah that's what I'd guess. It's hard to tell in here."

"If we came that far we should be near the top of the hill."

"Yeah, and I've been thinking another thing. Both times we had a choice we took the right turn. That means we might be in the next valley."

Anton turned and looked back at Paul.

"You mean we might be inside that fence?"

"I'm not saying we are, but we might be."

"If Patrick goes out of the tunnel they might shoot him."

"We don't know if we're inside the fence for one thing and they might not even see him if he does go out."

"Patrick! Come on boy!"

"Let's keep going," Paul said.

They moved forward. Now it was getting harder to go because the tunnel was getting too small for them. They weren't sure how much farther they could go.

"Smell that?" Anton said.

Paul sniffed the air.

"Smoke," he said. "Like a campfire."

"The outside must be close," Anton said.

They started down the tunnel toward the smoke smell. Suddenly they heard something ahead of them. Anton shined the light down the tunnel and they could see the eyes of an animal glowing in the light.

"What the?"

The eyes moved toward them. Anton backed up and ran into Paul.

"Something's coming," he said urgently.

Paul was partially blocked from the light by Anton's body. He could see the animal.

"It's Patrick," he said happily.

"Patrick! Come here boy," Anton said patting his chest.

The dog came running up to them and jumped up into Anton's arms. He was wagging his tail happily.

"What's he carrying?" Paul asked.

Anton grabbed the dog's head and took a leather work-glove from his mouth.

"Where did you get this?"

"He must have been outside the cave. I bet there's an angry Mexican missing a glove," Paul said.

"It looks like a mate to the other one he found," Anton said.

"Oh boy, I bet somebody is pissed that their gloves are missing."

"Let's get out of here," Anton said. "I've had enough of caves for one day."

He handed Paul the light and they turned and crawled back to where they'd come from. Patrick trotted along happily with them.

When they got to the end, they crawled out into the daylight. They both had to shield their eyes from the bright sun. Patrick grabbed at the glove and wanted to play fetch with it.

"I wonder if he stole that from one of those guys?" Anton said.

"He's lucky they didn't shoot him. We'll have to keep an eye on him from now on. Now that he's been through the cave he'll think it's a fun thing to do."

"Patrick, no." Anton held up the glove.

Patrick lunged forward and grabbed it and ran off.

"A lot of good that did," he said

Chapter 30

They hiked down to the Mule. Anton picked up the first glove from the back of the vehicle and compared the two gloves.

"It's the mate to the first one," he said holding the gloves up so Paul could see.

"Man, we've got to keep him close from now on. Somebody up in that valley is probably missing their gloves and if they see him up there they'll shoot him."

"Patrick, no."

Anton held the gloves by the dog and scolded him. He lunged and grabbed one and ran off with it.

"He thinks it's a game," Paul said.

"No kidding. Well we have to make sure he's right with us when we're up here. Man it's hot out here. After being in that cave it really feels like a sauna out here."

"You're right about that. Looking at you, I can see we're both covered with dirt and mud too. How about taking a swim?"

"Hey, good idea."

They walked to the beach and stripped off their dirty clothes. When they got to their boxers they decided to swim nude and then they could wear their dry boxers afterward on the trip home. They both jumped into the water at the same time.

"Yeeeeeooow!" Anton yelled as he came to the surface.

"Cold, cold!" Paul said.

Suddenly there was a splash and Patrick jumped off the bank and landed between them. They began splashing and playing with the dog and had a fine time once they got used to the cool water.

"It's gonna storm," Paul said looking to the west.

Anton looked and there were big banks of black clouds building up on the western horizon.

"Oh no," he said.

"It's just a summer storm. We haven't really had any storms all summer. These are pretty common."

"It looked just like that when... when it happened."

"You mean, when the tornado came?"

Anton nodded. "Let's get out."

They waded out of the water and wiped themselves as dry as they could. They slipped on their boxers and piled their dirty clothes in the back of the Mule. It was really hot and humid so they warmed up really quickly.

"Let's go home," Anton said looking at the approaching storm.

"That's a long way off. It won't be here for a while."

"I want to be someplace safe."

Paul looked at his friend and could see he was very afraid.

"I understand. Come on Patrick, let's go."

Patrick jumped up in the Mule and they took off down the valley. When they got to the house Paul parked the Mule in the garage and they carried their stuff inside. The house was cool since the AC was on. They took turns in the shower and dressed in tee shirts and shorts. Patrick was napping on the couch when they finished.

"Maybe we should sleep in the basement tonight," Anton said as he looked out the window.

"We'll watch the weather on TV and see if they have any

warnings," Paul said.

As they watched the weather channel they noticed their dad and mom drive up. They carried in some groceries and his mom started dinner.

"Do you think we should sleep in the basement tonight?" Anton said to her as she cooked.

"In the basement? Why would we do that Sweetie?"

"The storm is coming."

She understood then. "We'll watch really close and keep an eye on it. If we think we need to go to the basement, we can be down there in a minute."

He seemed okay with that. She hugged him.

"Anton, the odds of another tornado coming up this valley are a million to one. Your old house stood here for a hundred years and nothing happened to it until that day two years ago. The odds are in our favor."

"I know but I just can't forget. I lost everything that night. I said goodnight to my parents and never saw them again. I don't even know where they're buried."

"Oh my God. No one ever took you to their graves?"

He shook his head no.

"I suppose because I wasn't talking, no one thought I was fit to go."

"Do you want to go there?"

He nodded.

"Well I'll see what I can find out and you can visit them."

She put her arms around the boy and stroked his hair.

"We'll keep you safe, I promise."

Thunder and lightning began flashing in the west about dusk. The closer the storm got, the more the sky lit up and the thunder rumbled down the valley. Anton was glued to the weather channel. The forecast was for heavy rains and some wind but no tornados were expected.

"It's getting late," Paul said.

"Maybe I'll sit up and be sure."

"Anton, we're okay. There are no watches or warnings. They know pretty much about these things now days."

"I won't be able to sleep anyway," Anton said.

Paul sat there and looked at his friend. "Come with me."

He got up and shut off the TV. Then they went to their bedroom and Paul pulled the mattress off his bed. They took some blankets and their pillows and carried the whole works down to the basement. Paul made them a bed on the floor in the corner next to the laundry room.

"There, is that okay?"

Anton grinned. "Will you stay here too?"

"Yup."

"I'll take Patrick out and then we'll be good."

The dog and Anton sprinted up the stairs. They went to the front yard and Anton stood on the porch and watched as Patrick sniffed to find the right place. He watched the lightning and listened to the thunder. His heart was beating hard. Every time the lightning lit the sky he expected to see the monster coming at him across the valley. He was happy when Patrick came to him. He hurried back down to the basement.

Paul lay down on the mattress and soon Patrick came running down the stairs. Anton was right behind him.

"It just started raining."

"Come on, let's get some sleep."

Anton lay on one side of the mattress and Paul on the other with Patrick in between them.

They pulled a blanket up over them. Patrick wiggled around until he found his spot and then settled down.

"Paul?"

"Yeah?"

"Thanks."

"No problem."

Outside the storm hit. Rain came down in sheets and the wind whipped the trees and blew anything up into the valley that wasn't fastened down or very heavy. Lightning flashed in the basement windows lighting up the room.

Suddenly Paul sniffed.

"Patrick!"

Anton started laughing.

"Was that you?" Paul asked.

"Sorry. I'm very nervous."

"God, what a pig!"

Anton laughed for quite a while and then he slept.

Chapter 31

T he sun was shining into the basement through the little window in the foundation. The storm had passed and they weren't blown away.

Paul woke and looked over at Anton who was still sleeping. He smiled as he looked at the kid. He looked like a choirboy, with his hair hanging down over his forehead and baby face but he was a little mischievous too.

Patrick woke and saw Paul was awake and began wagging his tail. That woke Anton. He looked up and then out the window.

"All is well," he said smiling.

"It was just a summer storm."

"Yeah, I know. I'm a bit more cautious than you are. But you've never taken a ride on a tornado like I have."

"Yeah I can understand how you don't want to repeat that," Paul said. "Do you remember much of it?"

"I remember it happened so fast. One minute Patrick and I were in the tent and the next minute it was pitch dark and we were flying through the air. It seemed like we were flying around forever but it was probably only a few seconds. There was dirt and sticks and all kinds of stuff whirling around and hitting me. Patrick was barking frantically and I think I was screaming. Then something smashed my elbow and my arm went numb. I couldn't keep my hold on Patrick and he... he flew off into the darkness."

He stopped talking and shut his eyes.

"The next thing I knew I hit the ground. I was kind of semi-conscious and at first I thought I was dead. Then I felt the cold water on my back and knew I wasn't dead. I tried to move but nothing worked. I called and called for Patrick. I expected that he'd landed with me and would be there by me soon. But he never came. I never saw him again."

Paul hugged the kid.

"You're one in a million Anton," he said.

"The boy who fell from the sky," Anton said.

"You knew they called you that?"

He nodded.

"I wasn't talking. But that didn't mean I couldn't hear them talking."

"I don't think they meant anything by it."

"No I didn't take it badly. I knew I was pretty lucky."

"Well all that's past now."

"I wonder if those gloves that Patrick found came from those Mexican guys up in the valley?" Anton asked.

"I'd bet on it. I wish we knew what they were up to. It makes me nervous to think that they're up there with guns."

"I wonder how many of them there are?" Anton asked.

"Well we saw that one guy twice and each time he had a different guy with him so there are at least three of them."

"They're up to something," Anton said. "I'd be willing to bet on it."

"Let's take a drive up past there after Mom and Dad leave for work. The road goes past up to the ridge and then it splits and one way goes to town and the other goes to another town west of here."

"Maybe we can see something from up on the ridge," Anton suggested.

Paul showered while Anton took Patrick out for a pee. Paul was finished when they got back so Anton jumped into the shower and Paul went to the kitchen.

"Where were you guys last night?" his mom asked.

"Anton was uneasy with the storm so we slept in the

basement."

She smiled.

"He'll get over that after a while. I can understand him being a little scared."

"So how is the pond coming?" Paul's dad asked as he came to the kitchen.

"We're nearly finished. The dam is really well built. It will last a long time. The pond is full and the overflow is going out over a low spot in the dam. We're going to finish up the campsite soon and then we can have a cookout up there."

"Are there any fish in that pond?"

"Probably not many. There might be a few trout or suckers. I don't think the stream has much for fish."

"I'll ask around and see if anyone around here raises fish of some kind. If they do I'll see about buying some and we can stock it."

"Stock what?" Anton said coming into the room. He was barefoot and his hair was still wet.

"Dad is going to see about getting some fish for the pond."

"Cool. That'd be really good. Hey I just thought of something."

He turned to their dad.

"Why would the stream run really slowly sometimes? Some days there is just a trickle of water coming down the hill. Then it speeds up and runs fast for a day or so."

"Hmm. Somebody must be damming it up or pumping water from it. I don't know any other reason that would make it run slow."

"You think somebody is using water from it for irrigation?" Paul asked.

"That could be a reason."

"You guys stay away from that place," their mom said. "If their signs warn you away with a gun, you guys don't need to be anywhere near them."

"We'll stay away," Paul said.

They ate breakfast and the boys cleaned up so their parents could leave for work. Then they walked out to the Mule. Patrick jumped up in the carrier box and began playing with the gloves he'd stolen.

Anton took one of them and looked it over.

"Look here," he said pointing to the label. "It's in Spanish. These came from Mexico."

"It doesn't mean Mexico for certain," Paul said. "They might be from Honduras or some other South American country."

"Well either way they're not locals," Anton said.

"So that fits. Those guys look Hispanic and they have stuff from somewhere where Spanish is the language. They're up to something."

"Let's drive up past there and see what we can see."

"Right, let's go."

They jumped in the Mule and Patrick wagged his tail happily as they drove down the lane and then turned up on the road past the upper farm. They were very close to the gate when Patrick began barking. Anton looked over his shoulder and Patrick was barking at something in the ditch behind them.

"He sees something in the ditch," he said.

"Probably a rabbit or something."

"Patrick, shut up."

Patrick barked even louder. He began to climb over the truck box.

"Patrick sit down you'll fall out!"

Paul slowed down and the dog jumped out and ran back down the road.

"What the heck?" Paul said.

"Back up, let's see what he'd doing."

Paul backed up and they stopped. Patrick was standing next to a dog that was lying in the weeds. It looked like a collie mix.

Anton got out and walked over by them.

"Be careful, he might be dangerous," Paul said.

Anton walked very slowly and knelt down by the dog.

"Hey boy, what's wrong?"

The dog whined and tried to get up. He couldn't raise himself up.

"Paul he's hurt."

Paul shut off the Mule and got out. They walked down into the ditch. Patrick was very excited and seemed to be worried about the dog. Paul squatted down and petted it on the head.

"What's wrong?" he asked.

"Look he's got blood on his back leg."

Paul looked and sure enough, the dog's leg was covered with blood and had a wrong looking angle to it.

"He's been hit by a car or something," Paul said.

"We gotta help him."

"Of course we can't leave him lay. Let's see if we can pick him up. Be ready to get back. He might bite if we hurt him."

Paul took the front shoulders of the dog and Anton lifted very carefully on his rear end. The dog whined loudly like it was in a lot of pain but it didn't bite at them. They carried it up out of the ditch and laid it in the truck box.

Anton jumped up next to it.

"I'll ride back here and keep it steady," he said.

Patrick jumped up and sat next to the dog. He looked worried.

"Hang on we'll head for the Vet."

Chapter 32

Anton petted the dog's head as they drove down the road. He looked it over and it was a mix of some kind. His hair was longish and had the coloring of a golden retriever but it's face looked more like a collie. It was thin and looked pretty rough.

"You're okay now," he said quietly.

The dog looked up at him and licked his hand. It had soft brown eyes and even though it was in pain and nearly starved, it was very friendly.

They got to town and drove to the Vet's office. Paul ran inside and soon he emerged with one of the Vets, carrying a stretcher.

"You said you guys lifted him up?"

"Yeah, he whined but didn't try to bite us," Anton said.

"Let's see if we can get him on the stretcher."

They lifted the dog carefully and he began whining. He was obviously in pain. They got him on the stretcher and Paul and the Vet. carried him to the office. Anton stayed with Patrick who was very nervous.

"You did good Patrick," Anton said petting the dog. "You probably saved that dog's life."

Just then Paul came out and motioned for Anton to come in.

"What about Patrick?"

"Bring him... its a Vet's office."

Anton and Patrick walked in and followed Paul to an examining room.

"Well we can start calling him, her," the Vet said. "This is a female dog."

"Can you tell what's wrong?"

"I've cleaned the wound a bit but I'd say she's been shot. It looks like she has a bullet hole in her hip."

"Oh my gosh," Anton said. "Will she be okay?"

"Well I need to take an X-ray to be sure. But I think I can fix her up. The problem is it will be somewhat expensive. Do you know who owns this dog?"

"We found her along the road," Paul said.

"What happens to her if she doesn't get fixed up?"

"Well unless we can find an owner, I'd probably have to put her down. I know it sounds heartless but we have to pay bills here too. I'm going to check her for a microchip."

He got a device and passed it over the dog. Nothing happened.

"What was that?" Anton asked.

"Many people now days have a chip implanted in their dog in case they get lost or stolen and that chip can be read by that device. This dog has no chip."

Paul looked at Anton and they both knew what was going to happen.

"Can I have a minute to make a call?" Paul asked.

"Take your time. The bleeding is stopped so she's okay for now. But she needs attention soon. I gave her a pain shot so she's not in so much pain now."

Paul stepped out into the hall and called his mother. He explained the situation with the dog.

"What will happen to the dog if she recovers?" his mom asked.

"Well I guess we'd have to find a home for her."

"You know how that will end up."

"Mom, she's a sweet dog. It's not her fault someone shot her. We'll ask around and maybe put an ad in the paper and try and find her owner."

"I suppose Anton is already in love with her," his mom said.

Paul looked into the exam room. Anton was sitting an a stool next to the dog stroking it's head. Patrick sat beside him looking up and looking very worried.

"I think he and Patrick are pretty fond of her already."

"Oh man. Well write my credit card number down and use it. Call me to let me know how it comes out."

"Will you call Dad?"

"Yeah I'll call him. He'll be fine with it. He loves Patrick already. Another dog will be fine with him."

Paul stepped into the room and held his thumb up.

"My mom will pay... fix her up."

The Vet went to ready the X-ray machine and Anton picked up Patrick so he could see the other dog. Patrick licked her on the face and her tail wagged.

"See they're friends already," Anton said.

"We'll have to give her a name," Paul said.

"Sandy," Anton said.

"Sandy? That's a good name. Why did you choose that?"

Anton looked up at Paul. His eyes filled with tears.

"My Mom. That was her name."

Paul put his arms around the boy.

"Then Sandy it will be," he said quietly.

Twenty minutes later the Vet came and motioned for them to follow him. He took them to the X-ray room and showed them the picture of Sandy's leg.

"You can see here, the bullet passed through her femur, the upper bone in her leg. It went through and didn't do any damage to anything else. We can open the leg up and we'll have to put a steel rod in to support the bone where the bullet damaged it. But she should heal up fine. You'll have to help her for a while, getting up and down. She's also very emaciated. She must have been on her own for a long time. She's about twenty pounds underweight for the size of a dog that she is. Of course that is good now with the leg but she'll need to feed up and gain some weight."

"We can do all of that," Anton said.

"Well then, we'll get started on the surgery. It will take an hour or so. She'll need to be in recovery for a few hours so I'd say come back about mid-afternoon and she'll be ready to go."

The boys thanked the Doc and left. The got in the Mule but Patrick was very upset that they were leaving Sandy behind. Anton tried to explain to him but it didn't help.

"Let's take him to Taco Bell. That will settle him down."

They went and ate and then went to Walmart and got a new bed for Sandy and more dog food.

Paul called his mom and told her the news. She said their dad was happy they'd stopped and helped the dog.

"So what can we do now for a few hours?" Paul asked.

"There's someplace I'd like to go," Anton said.

"Where is that?"

"Well, when the tornado killed my parents and Old Patrick I was in the hospital with my back broken. I didn't get to go to their funeral and then I went to the nursing home and I've never seen their graves."

"Oh my gosh, I had no idea," Paul said.

"If it isn't too much trouble," Anton said.

"Do you know where they're buried?"

Anton shook his head.

Chapter 33

"No one told you where your parents were buried?" Paul asked.

"I was a thirteen year old kid who didn't talk. I guess no one thought to tell me."

"Well there must be somebody who knows. I'm going to call Mom and find out who they talked to about buying the land where we live."

Paul called his mother and she gave him the name of a lawyer who handled the sale of the land. Paul looked the guy up in the phone book and found his address, so the boys drove over to the office.

"Patrick, you stay," Anton said to the dog as they got out of the Mule.

Patrick sat down and wagged his tail.

They walked into the office and up to a counter where a lady sat.

"How may I help you?"

Paul explained the situation and she said she would be right back. She walked down a hallway and soon came back.

"Mr. Jonas has a few minutes, you can go right in."

They entered the office and a tall man wearing a suit got up from behind the desk and shook hands with both of them.

"Well I must say you look fit," he said to Anton.

"You know me?"

"We never really met. I was appointed by the county to be your legal guardian when you were hurt. I looked in on you at the hospital but you were sleeping. You looked a bit worse for wear when I saw you last. I'm glad to see you've recovered from your ordeal."

"Thank you. I didn't know how everything was done. I was kind of out of it."

"That's understandable. Since you were and still are a minor, I'm your legal guardian. I have oversight on your estate and manage your money."

"What money? I don't have any money."

"Oh you have a substantial sum of money Anton. The county ordered the land sold since you were a minor and couldn't pay the taxes. So I sold it to Paul's parents. Then life insurance and homeowner's insurance paid you a substantial amount. It's all in a Trust that you will be able to obtain when you turn 18."

"I didn't know anything about that," the boy said.

"You'll be set up pretty well Anton. Your parents thought ahead and when you turn legal age your education and your future are very solid."

Anton lowered his head. "I'd rather have Mom and Dad and Patrick."

Paul put his hand on Anton's shoulder and squeezed it.

"Well things being as they are, what else can I do for you?"

"I wondered if you know where they're buried."

"No one ever took you to their graves?"

"No."

The lawyer got up and pulled a file from a cabinet. He paged through it and then wrote something down on a paper. He handed Anton the paper.

"That's the cemetery and their plot number. The cemetery is on the east side of town. Go there and ask the attendant and he'll give you a map to show you where they are."

Anton and Paul got up and thanked the man.

"Anything you need Anton. Any time. You call me and I'll be here for you," the man said.

They drove to the cemetery and found an old man who was working on a lawn mower. Anton showed him the paper and he went inside the building and got a map and made an X on it.

"Thank you," Anton said.

"If you can't find it, come back and I'll help you," the old man said.

"Is it okay if we take Patrick?"

"Sure no problem."

They got Patrick from the Mule. Then they walked down a road and took a right on another and soon they found the grave. Paul stood back and let Anton go to the grave alone.

He stood there looking down at his Mom and Dad's names on the slab of granite. He could picture them in his mind, smiling and laughing with him. Tears came to his eyes and he knelt in the grass by the grave.

Patrick scampered over to him and he picked up the dog and buried his face in his fur.

"This is where they are," he said. "You would have liked them."

The dog licked his face.

Paul walked over and knelt by Anton.

"Are you okay?"

He nodded. "Now I know where they are. I know where Old Patrick is too."

"I'm sorry Anton. I know how I'd feel in your place."

Anton turned and hugged Paul.

"I know they'd like you. I'm sure they're watching out for us."

They got up and walked back to the Mule.

"Well let's go and see how Sandy is doing."

When they got to the Vet's office they went in and were taken to a room with several wire cages lined up against the wall. Sandy was in one of them lying on a blanket. Her hip was bandaged up and she had a shaved place on her left front leg. She was sleeping.

"So how did it go?" Paul asked.

"It went well. The bullet went through the bone and shattered it but didn't do much damage and went right on out. It must have been a .22. We cleaned up the bone chips and put a steel rod in and she should be just fine. You'll have to keep her quiet for a week or so but I think she'll recover back to her old self. She needs to be fed some good high protein food to get her back to weight and you have to watch for infections. I gave her a general worm killer so that should help her to gain some weight."

"When can we take her home?"

"She's ready to go. One of you will have to carry her. She's still a bit loopy on the drugs."

They knelt down by the cage and opened it. Sandy opened her eyes and looked at them and then she jumped back like she was frightened.

The Vet laughed.

"She's not afraid of you. She's seeing pink bunnies or something from the anesthetic. Dogs always do that when they're waking up."

They got her out of the cage and Paul lifted her up. She wasn't much heavier than Patrick but she was a much larger dog. She was so skinny she didn't weigh much. They thanked the Doctor and carried her out to the Mule.

Patrick was very excited when he saw her. Anton got in the cargo box in back and Paul laid the dog on the floor of the box with her head on Anton's lap. Patrick jumped in next to Anton and sniffed Sandy.

"Be gentle," Anton said.

Patrick's talk was wagging like mad.

They pulled out and started home. Paul looked over his shoulder and Anton was smiling and petting Sandy with one hand and Patrick with the other.

"Oh boy," Paul thought.

Chapter 34

They drove slowly back home so Sandy didn't get jostled too much. When they got home the parents came out to meet their new dog. Anton held her in his lap in the back of the Mule and Patrick wagged his tail excitedly as they walked up.

They both petted the dog that was now fully awake. She seemed like she was a little overwhelmed at all the humans around her. Paul got the new dog bed and stuff from the passenger seat and his dad carried it inside the house. Paul picked Sandy out of Anton's lap and carried her to the yard. He put her down gently so she could go potty if she needed to.

The dog looked around and then limped on three legs a little way off and squatted and peed.

"She pees like Patrick," Anton said.

Then the dog looked around and started off towards the woods. Paul ran over to her.

"Hey, where are you going Sandy?"

The dog looked up. Obviously she figured she was still on her own and was going to look for someplace to rest and hopefully something to eat.

"You come with me," Paul said patting his leg.

She stood there a bit and then hobbled after him. When she got to the steps leading up on the porch Paul leaned down and picked her up. He carried her into the kitchen/dining room and laid her on the new dog bed they'd bought for her. She lay there looking around.

"I'll get her something to eat," Anton said.

He filled her food bowl with dog food and one with water and put them by her. She looked at the food and then got up shakily and began eating. She ate like it was her first meal in a long time.

Patrick sat and watched her, wagging his tail.

Paul told his parents about Sandy being shot.

"You say you found her up by the next farm in the road?"

"Yeah, she was in the ditch. I bet those Mexican guys shot her. We hear them shooting up there all the time."

"I wonder what they're up to?" his mom said.

His dad didn't say anything but he had a worried look on his face.

They ate dinner and Anton fed both of the dogs little tidbits from his plate. Sandy was very excited to get people food.

After dinner they went outside and sat on the porch. Sandy limped around in the grass for a while and then pooped. Then she lay down on the lawn and Patrick hauled all of his toys over by her.

"She can't play yet Patrick," Anton said. He went over and threw the ball for the dog and he ran and retrieved it. Sandy watched and wagged her tail.

"She seems to be friendly," their mom said.

"Yeah, I think she got lost or somebody dumped her and she made the mistake of wandering into the Mexican's place. You're sure it's okay for us to keep her?" Paul asked.

"What's one more dog? We got a new kid, and two new dogs in no time since moving here. I can't wait to see what turns up next," Paul's dad said.

After an hour it started getting dark so they all went inside. The boys said goodnight and went to their room. They carried Sandy's bed into the bedroom. They both showered and then Anton got in bed and Patrick jumped up and snuggled down next to him.

Paul came back from the shower and got in his bed. Sandy was in her dog bed by the side of his bed.

Paul shut off the light. There was a lot of moonlight streaming in from the window. Soon he noticed Sandy's face on the edge of the bed. She was standing looking up at him.

"What?"

"She wants up," Anton said from across the room. Paul could see he was grinning.

Paul sighed. He got up and lifted the dog into his bed. She watched him get back in bed and then she circled around three times and lay down next to him. She took a deep breath and let out a long sigh. She was home.

Chapter 35

Paul woke when he felt a constant thumping on the bed. He opened his eyes and Sandy was lying on the bed next to him with her head on the other pillow, looking at him. When his eyes opened the thumping increased.

"Good morning," he said quietly. "Did you have a good sleep?"

The dog wiggled and was very excited.

Paul petted her head.

"You're a good girl. I bet you have to go potty," he said.

The dog tried to get up but struggled.

"Let me help you," Paul said and he got up and lifted the dog to the floor. She made her way toward the door on three legs and he opened the door and they went to the front of the house. He opened the front door and the dog hopped down the steps to the lawn and squatted.

Paul stood there watching her. She looked a lot better today. She was getting around much easier and she seemed to have a lot more strength.

Suddenly the door opened and Anton and Patrick came hustling through. Patrick hurried to the lawn and ran to a tree, lifted his leg and peed.

"Holy cow, he's peeing like a boy," Anton said proudly.

"Maybe he saw Sandy pee and decided he better be more manly," Paul suggested.

They watched as Patrick sprinted over by Sandy. The two dogs tails wagged furiously and they sniffed each other. Then they walked around the yard and it looked like Patrick was showing her his kingdom.

"You guys want some breakfast?"

The boys turned and saw their mom standing in the doorway.

"You bet," Anton said.

They called the dogs. Patrick bounded up the steps and then waited for Sandy to work her way up. She got along pretty well on three legs but was just slower and more methodical in her walking.

The boys went and dressed and when they came back to the kitchen there was a stack of pancakes on the table along with a plate of sausages. Their dad was sitting waiting for them. The dogs were lying on the floor next to the table.

"She looks a lot better today," Paul's dad said.

"She slept on my bed with me," Paul said grinning.

His mom shook her head.

"Why doesn't that surprise me?"

"Well she is part of the family now. If Patrick gets to sleep on a bed she should too," Paul said.

"So what are you two doing today?" Chuck asked.

"We haven't really thought about it," Paul said.

"We should set up our campsite. Then we can cut some firewood and sleep up there one of these night," Anton said.

"If you get real ambitious, you can cut some firewood for the fireplace for next winter," Chuck said.

"There's enough fire wood for twenty years on the opposite hillside where the tornado went," Paul said.

He saw Anton stop eating for a second and was sorry he'd mentioned the tornado.

Anton looked up.

"Hey it's okay. We can't keep sidestepping the past. What happened is past. The chances of another tornado are what... astronomical?"

"One in a million at least," Paul said.

"Well, that's pretty good odds."

Their parents left for work and the boys made some

sandwiches and packed a cooler. They loaded up in the Mule with Sandy lying in the back and drove up to the pond. Paul lifted Sandy out onto the ground and she and Patrick walked off checking things out. The boys unloaded the tent and got the instructions out.

"Holy cow, this is a puzzle," Anton said trying to sort out the poles and ropes.

"Well, let's take our time and get it right. We don't want it falling down in the middle of the night."

They cleared off a spot big enough for the tent and took an old broom and swept it clear of all rocks and other stuff that would make a lump in the floor. They worked for nearly an hour and finally they had the tent up and all ready to go. It was a fine tent and big enough for the two of them, the dogs and a lot of extra stuff.

"This is like a palace," Anton said. "It's way better than the one I had."

They went back to the house for their cots and blankets and other gear, hauled it up to the pond and set it all up. When they were finished they stood back and looked at their campsite.

"Pretty darn nice," Paul said.

"All we need is a TV and we could live here."

They ate their lunch and shared it with the dogs. Patrick had been sniffing around most of the time but Sandy laid and watched them for the most part.

After lunch they lay back on a blanket on the sandy beach and rested.

"I wonder how cold the water is?" Anton said.

"Go stick your toe in it," Paul answered.

Anton grinned and got up. He kicked off his flip-flop and stuck his foot into the water. He grinned.

"It's nice,"

"Really? You sure?"

"Yeah, it's really nice. It might be a little chilly but not too bad."

"Want to go for a swim?"

"Yeah lets."

Paul jumped up and stripped off his shirt and shorts. He kicked off his flip-flops while Anton was still taking off his shorts.

"Hurry up," he said.

"Go ahead, I'm right behind you."

Paul went up on the bank and took a run toward the pond. When he was at the edge he jumped as far out as he could and landed with a splash in the water. He went under and came up like a breeching whale.

"Holy crap!"

Anton was laughing his head off.

"It's freezing!"

"It felt okay on my foot."

"Well I got more than my foot wet. Get in here."

"You know, I decided I'm not feeling like a swim just now," Anton said grinning.

"Oh? We'll see about that."

Paul swam to the shore and Anton took off running. Paul was right behind him. Patrick ran behind Paul barking crazily and Sandy barked and hobbled along behind him.

"You're going in," Paul huffed.

"No way, you'll never catch me."

They went up the hill and then Anton turned and headed farther up the valley. Paul was right behind him. Anton looked over his shoulder and saw that Paul was catching up. He made a fake to the left and then turned right and headed back toward the Mule. Paul took the fake and spun out and landed in the grass on his butt.

Anton got a little lead and wasn't far from the Mule. He stopped to jump on it and Paul came from the side and tackled him. They rolled down the bank and into the pond. Anton came up screaming.

"Help, help, he's drowning me!"

"Yell all you want you little shit. There's no one to hear you."

Anton started swimming away but Paul grabbed him and pushed his head under water. Then Paul climbed out on the bank. Anton came to the top laughing and climbed out behind him.

"You turd," he said. "You nearly drowned me."

Paul grinned. "You're lucky. I should have held you under for a while."

They were both shivering. Paul was wearing his boxers but Anton was fully wet in all his clothes.

"Too bad you don't have anything dry to change into," Paul said.

"Yeah too bad," Anton said.

Patrick was jumping around thinking it was a wonderful game and Sandy was sitting a little way off.

"She must be tired out," Paul said. He walked to the dog and picked her up.

"You need a lift girl?"

Just then he heard the Mule start. Anton was wearing Paul's shorts and shirt and he waved as he drove off toward the house. Patrick was standing in the box wagging his tail.

"I'll get you!" Paul said.

He watched as Anton drove off.

"Well I guess we have to walk home," he said.

He carried the dog and walked along in his wet boxers, barefoot.

"That little fart," he said under his breath.

Then he grinned. The kid had come a long way from that sad little boy who wouldn't speak a few weeks ago.

"Still... I will get revenge," he said.

Chapter 36

The boys hauled a cooler full of food and drinks, a radio and some clothes up to the pond. They also hauled up the chainsaw and a can of gas. They wore jeans and leather boots and walked up on the hillside where the tornado had knocked down hundreds of trees and began cutting them into firewood.

Paul had run a chainsaw before so he cut the wood and Anton rolled the pieces down the hill to the bottom where they'd load them onto the Mule and haul them home. They had a good bunch of wood cut, so they took a break for a soda.

"Can I try the saw?" Anton asked.

"Sure, you just have to be careful."

They rested for a bit and then Anton cut his first piece of firewood. It went well so he continued. They sawed up seven trees and had quite a large bunch of wood rolled down the hill.

"Let's quit cutting for a while and go and haul some home," Paul suggested.

They hiked down to the Mule and loaded the back with wood. Patrick stood on top of the load and Sandy road up front with them. They took it slow back to the house. The Mule was pretty well loaded down.

The piled the smaller wood next to the garage. They piled the thicker stuff that needed to be split in another pile. When they were unloaded they went back for a second load and then a third. When they finished with that one they decided they'd done enough work for the day. They both showered and then they went up to the pond to sit and rest.

"This is a really cool spot," Paul said as they sat in lawn chairs sipping a soda.

Just then they heard several shots from the upper farm behind the fence. Sandy whined and cowered.

"Look at her. She's scared. I bet anything that those guys up there are the ones who shot her," Anton said.

"I wonder what they're shooting at?"

Anton just shook his head.

When it got close to dinnertime they put the chairs and other stuff in the tent and zipped it up. Then they drove down to the house and had brats on the grill with their parents.

"That's a nice pile of wood," Chuck said.

"We've got a bunch more cut. We can burn wood for years from all that's up there," Paul said.

"When you guys get done hauling wood down, we can rent a splitter from the garden-center and split that thick stuff up," their dad said.

"Yeah, that sounds like a good plan," Paul said.

"We heard a bunch of shooting up in the valley," Anton said.

Chuck looked uneasy.

"I asked around and no one knows what's going on up there. I think I have an idea but I hate to say what I think."

"Drugs?" Paul asked.

His dad nodded.

"I think it might be a pot farm."

"What can we do about it?"

"We can do nothing. You guys stay away from it. I'm going to talk to the sheriff and see if they know anything. But I repeat, you guys stay out of there."

"Do you think they'd shoot us?" Anton asked.

"I don't want to find out. If it's a pot farm they have guards, and who knows what kind of security. The farther away from that place that you are, the better off you are."

The boys promised they'd stay away.

It was getting dusk when Paul suggested they sleep in the tent for the night. It was a beautiful summer night so they loaded up, said goodnight to the parents and drove the Mule up to the pond.

They lit their lantern and made a fire in their fire pit. By the time they had the fire going it was dark. They sat and watched the fire and talked late into the night.

"I think Dad is right. I bet those guys are up there growing pot," Paul said.

"Why would they do it here in Wisconsin? Don't they usually do it someplace that's warmer for a longer time?"

"I don't know for sure, but I think if they can find a remote place they'll grow it anywhere. Plus if they grow it here, they don't have to worry about smuggling it across the border."

Anton looked up into the dark valley.

"It'd be interesting to see what's going on wouldn't it?"

Paul grinned.

"Not interesting enough to get shot."

"True."

The fire was dying so they walked off into the dark and both peed and then they crawled into the tent. They took off their shoes and socks and shorts and crawled into their sleeping bags. The two dogs lay down beside their masters. Sandy snuggled up right next to Paul.

"She decided you're her man," Anton said smiling.

"I've never had a dog but I kinda like having her with me

like this. She's a sweet girl."

"She's a lucky girl. If we hadn't driven past, she'd probably be lying in that ditch and be nothing but bones by now," Anton said.

They shut off the light.

"Good night," Paul said.

"Good night."

They were both just about asleep when they heard three shots come from the upper valley.

Chapter 37

T he boys overslept the next morning and missed getting back to the house for breakfast. Their parents were already gone to work so they settled for toast and cereal.

"Let's make some more firewood today," Paul said.

"Yeah, that sounds like a good idea. Actually I like doing that. It doesn't seem much like work and it's kind of enjoyable."

They dressed in leather boots and jeans and drove the Mule up the valley and up onto the hillside with all the downed trees. Paul fired up the chainsaw and as he cut wood, Anton carried it to the Mule. They had a load in no time and hauled it to the house where they stacked it.

Then they went back for another load.

"Let's move up there," Anton said pointing.

Paul nodded.

"That's a big pile of logs. We can cut there for a long time and not have to move very much."

They parked the Mule next to a tangle of trees and branches that had fallen into a jumbled mess. Paul began working on the outside of the pile cutting branches into firewood lengths while Anton carried them to the Mule. The two dogs sniffed and explored.

They had the Mule filled a second time and looked for the dogs. They were nowhere to be seen.

"There they are," Paul said pointing deep into the pile of logs.

"Hey Patrick, come here," Anton called.

Both of the dogs were sniffing around under a bunch of branches and their tails were wagging fast.

"I wonder what they're doing?"

"It looks like they found something interesting."

"Yeah, look at their tails wagging."

The boys climbed through the tangle of branches and suddenly Anton saw what the dogs were looking at.

"Holy smokes, there's my dirt bike!"

Paul looked where he was pointing and he could see a part of something that was bright yellow at the bottom of the pile.

"Your dirt bike?"

"Yeah, I had a dirt bike and I'd ridden it up to the pond that night. When the wind began tearing everything apart it flew off into the dark. I guess it landed up here and the trees fell on top of it."

"Wow, I wonder if it still runs?"

Anton shrugged.

"It might, but we have to dig it out to find out."

Paul went back to the edge of the pile and got the chainsaw. Then he climbed back into the tangle and began cutting limbs away. Anton tossed the limbs out of the way and they slowly worked their way down to the bike.

They cut a hole through the limbs and tree trunks and got to where they could get to the bike, and shut off the saw. They pulled it up and could see it had been beaten up some but it didn't look beyond repair.

The handlebars were bent out of shape and the gas tank had a big dent in it. Both tires were still inflated but one fender was pretty bent up.

"I think we can fix this," Paul said.

"You think? Wow, that'd be great."

They stood there looking around.

"There's no way we can lift it out of here. We're going to have to cut a path to it," Paul said.

Anton nodded.

"It's been here for two years. I guess there's no hurry. Why don't we cut the wood into the pile and haul it like we've been doing. Then when we get to the bike we can wheel it out and see if we can get it fixed?"

Paul thought that was a great idea. They worked their way out of the pile and hauled the load they had on the Mule back to the house. It was past noon so they had some sandwiches.

"That bike looks like it would be fun to ride," Paul said.

"Oh it goes like crazy. I never told my parents but I had it up to sixty a few times. I had trails all over the hills too. I cut all the junk out of the way and even made jumps on them."

"Cool, I hope we can get it fixed, it'd be fun to do some trail riding."

"I had trails up to the upper farm too. Now with that fence we couldn't get to them but I know what the place looks like from riding up there."

"Hmm, that's interesting," Paul said.

"Let's go and get another load. If we clear out two or three more loads we'll be at the bike."

They cleaned up their lunch mess and headed back up to the hill. It took four more loads over the next two days to get to the bike. When they cut the last log from on top of the Kawasaki they were pretty impressed. It had landed on its side and the way the logs landed, they piled over it but none of them really landed on the bike itself. It was dented and was muddy but looked in pretty good shape.

"For flying through the air like a little airplane it looks pretty good," Anton said.

"Let's take that last load of wood and then come back for it," Paul said.

They hauled the wood down to the house and stacked it. Then they went back up and wheeled the bike out of the pile of logs. It looked pretty good for what it had been through.

They put it on the Mule and strapped it down. The dogs were very interested in it, sniffing it and wagging their tails.

"You guys did good," Anton said petting them.

They both seemed pretty excited.

When the got to the house their parents were home and they showed them the bike. Chuck was a lot more excited about it than Nancy was.

"There's a bike shop in town. I bet they can work on it and get it going," he said excitedly.

"That'd be cool," Anton said.

Nancy shook her head.

"It looks dangerous."

Chuck rolled his eyes.

"Moms," he said.

Chapter 38

Paul woke the next morning and looked over to see Anton and Patrick snuggled together sleeping. He petted Sandy and she looked up and yawned.

"Do you want to get up?" he said to the dog.

She buried her face in the blankets and he decided she wanted to sleep a while longer. He got up and went to the kitchen where his parents were eating breakfast.

"Paul did you know that today is Anton's birthday?" his mom asked.

"No he didn't say anything about it."

"Well I just happened to notice it on the papers we got from Social Services or we'd have forgotten it too. He's sixteen today."

"Wow, we should have a party," Paul said.

His parents smiled and nodded.

"We're going to get some presents for him and a cake. Can we pick up something from you?"

"Get him a helmet for his bike. You are getting it fixed aren't you?"

"I'm taking it to the shop today."

"Well let's hope they can fix it and then he'll have a helmet."

"Paul has Anton said anything about wanting to stay here permanently?" his mom asked.

"He really hasn't said anything but I think he likes it here and would love to stay."

The parents smiled and nodded. They had something cooked up.

Anton and the two dogs came hustling out of the bedroom. Anton was in his boxers and he was hurrying.

"Patrick let a fart and I think he's got to poop bad!" he said as they went past the kitchen. He opened the door and the two dogs ran to the yard. Patrick hunched up and dropped a big pile on the grass. Anton stood there grinning.

"He's a good boy," he said.

"Don't forget to clean up your good boy's present," Chuck said.

"No problem. Am I too late for breakfast?"

"No, get dressed and I'll make you something," Nancy said.

He hustled off to the bedroom and soon came back dressed in a tee shirt and shorts.

"So what's up?" he asked.

"Why would you think anything is up?" Paul asked.

"You guys look like you're keeping something a secret."

They all tried to look innocent.

"Nothing to hide."

Anton nodded. "Okay then."

Their parents left for work, and the two boys filled the chainsaw and Mule with gas and went to cut some more firewood. They were up on the hill and had a big bunch of trees cut up, and were loading it. Suddenly there were several shots from the upper farm.

They stood and watched but no one came from the woods.

"What the heck are they shooting at?" Paul asked.

"Dang I want to go up there," Anton said.

"No way, you'd get shot."

"I'm pretty quick," he said grinning.

"Not quicker than a bullet," Paul said.

Anton shrugged.

"I suppose not. One of these day though, we gotta find out

what they're doing."

"You know what curiosity did to the cat don't you?"

"What cat? Do we have a cat?"

Paul shook his head.

That evening the boys had been in the hot tub and were in their room getting dressed for dinner. Chuck was making steaks on the grill, so they wanted to be ready when the steaks were done. They ate outside at the picnic table and talked about the pile of firewood they were making and many other things.

"One of these days you guys need to go to the garden center and rent their wood splitter," Chuck said.

"How will we get it home?"

"It's on wheels. You can hook it to the Mule and pull it home. You can split that pile of big wood in no time with it."

"Cool, I've seen them on TV. They look like they'd be fun to play with," Anton said.

"They're dangerous. You have to be careful," Nancy said.

Chuck's phone rang and he took the call.

"Good we're ready," he said.

"Who was that?" Paul asked.

"It was the guy from the cycle shop. Anton's bike has a cracked motor block. It would cost nearly as much as a new bike to fix it."

Anton looked disappointed.

"Oh well, we have the Mule," Paul said.

"Yeah, I guess."

Just then a horn sounded out front. Chuck told Anton to go to the door and see whom it was. Nancy and Chuck motioned for Paul to stay with them.

"What's going on?" Paul asked.

"Just wait," his dad said grinning.

"No Way! Are you joking me? Mom, Dad, Paul come here!"

They got up and there stood Anton and the guy from the cycle shop. He was standing beside a brand new Kawasaki bike with a big red ribbon on it.

"This man says this is mine!"

"It is, happy birthday."

"Happy what? What's today?"

"Today is July 1st."

"Holy smokes, I'm sixteen today."

Nancy motioned to Paul and they went in the house and came back with half a dozen presents. Chuck thanked he guy from the cycle shop and he left.

"So there are some rules," Nancy said.

"Oh?"

"You must wear a helmet."

"Okay, I have to get one."

"Here," Paul said handing him a package.

Anton ripped it open and it held a bright red shiny helmet. He grabbed Paul and hugged him.

"Wow, thanks, oh wow."

"Can I take it for a spin?"

"You've got more presents," Nancy said.

"Just a little quick tryout."

Chuck grinned.

"I'll get the gas can."

They filled the bike with gas and Anton put his helmet on and started the bike. He was grinning from ear to ear as he eased it out of the yard. Patrick and Sandy followed him barking. When he got a little way from the house he opened it up and did a quick run up and down the valley.

"He's going awfully fast," Nancy said.

Chuck and Paul winked. They both knew he was holding back. Anton came back a few minutes later and the dogs came dragging in, exhausted.

"Wow, thanks so much," he said hugging each of them.

"We have more goodies," Nancy said.

Anton opened a bunch of presents and there was one last

one. He opened the flat box and there was a paper inside. He took it out and read it and his eyes filled with tears.

"Does this mean I'm really your son now?" he asked.

"It does. We've officially adopted you and for better or worse, we're your parents now, and Paul is your brother."

They all hugged. Anton looked at the paper again.

"It says Anton Sands-Daniels, is that my name now?"

"We had it done that way so you can go by that name or you can go by either of the two. We didn't want to try to make you forget your real parents or your past."

He nodded. "I think this is good. But you are my real parents from now on."

"Well, let's go inside. We have cake!"

Paul put his arm around Anton's shoulder on the way inside.

"Welcome brother," he said.

Anton nodded and some tears ran down his cheeks.

Chapter 39

"I'm going to ride my bike," Anton said as Paul got on the Mule the next morning. "You take the dogs."

The boys were going to cut wood again and Anton wanted to ride his new dirt bike in the worst way.

"Okay, let's go," Paul said.

He started up the Mule and the two dogs sat in back with their tongues out panting. Patrick looked back when he saw Anton wasn't with them but his tail wagged when his master came up behind them on the new bike.

Anton drove up next to them and then he revved up the bike and off he went, leaving them in his dust. He flew up the valley, made a wide turn and headed back toward them. Paul grinned as he saw how good Anton was on the bike. He was pretty surprised when the kid gunned the bike and popped a wheelie and went past him on one tire.

"Holy smokes!" he said to the dogs.

Soon Anton came back on one wheel and passed him, turning and gunning it up the hill to the spot where they had been cutting wood. He was standing next to the bike grinning when Paul pulled up.

"Don't you dare tell Mom and Dad I did that," he said.

"Wow, you're pretty good on that thing," Paul said.

"You should see me do jumps. I've got some good ramps on my trails. I go air born."

"I won't say anything but don't go too nuts. If you crash it Mom will take it away."

They cut wood and hauled three loads back to the house. Then they drove back up to the hill and Anton got his bike. Paul headed down the valley and watched as Anton rode down by the pond. He stopped at the dam and looked to see if Paul was watching. Then he lifted his hand and waved and rode the bike across the little road on top of the dam. Paul stopped the Mule and watched him, shaking his head.

"He's pretty darn brave," he said to the dogs.

Anton got on the other side and did a loop and headed back to the bridge. When he was about ten feet away he popped a wheelie and rode across the dam on one wheel.

Paul was still sitting with his mouth agape when he pulled up next to him.

"What do you think of that?"

"I think you're crazy in your head."

Anton laughed and off he went toward the house.

"We're about out of gas for the Mule and the bike," Paul said.

"Want to run into town and get some?"

"Sure," Paul said.

"We might have to run past KFC too."

"That too," Paul said.

They ate at KFC and then stopped at a gas station. They filled two gas cans in the back of the Mule, and then filled the Mule, and then went inside to pay. Anton noticed a cardboard display of flashlights on the counter and one of them was on.

"Somebody left your flashlight on," he said taking the light from the box.

"They don't have batteries, it doesn't matter," the man said.

"What?"

"They have a generator inside. All you do is shake them and they charge up. You shake for a minute and they shine for half an hour or more. Then you shake them again and you're good for another half hour."

The boys each picked up a flashlight and shook them. They had a LED light that shined really bright.

"They'd be perfect for the campsite," Anton said.

"And for the cave," Paul added.

They bought two of the lights, paid for the gas and headed home.

On the edge of town there was a pickup sitting along the road. There were banners were strung up on metal posts advertising fireworks.

"The 4th of July is this weekend," Anton said, "Let's get some fireworks."

Paul pulled in and they got out and looked over the stuff. They bought some Roman Candles and some bottle rockets.

"Do you have anything a little bigger?" Paul asked.

The guy looked around.

"Something with a little more pop?"

Paul nodded.

"I do have some M80's and some Cherry Bombs, but they're illegal to shoot off. I can sell them to you but you aren't allowed to shoot them," he said with a grin.

"Oh," Paul said. He looked at Anton who was grinning from ear to ear.

"They're just for looking," Anton said.

"Well then, how many do you want?" the guy asked.

They bought a box of two dozen of each.

"Just for looking?" Paul said as they drove away.

Anton shrugged.

"If one happens to fall close to an open fire, it sure isn't our fault."

About a mile before they got to their driveway they met the old blue pickup. The two Mexican guys were in it and the passenger looked surprised when he saw Sandy sitting in the back of the Mule. Their brake lights came on when they went past.

"They stopped," Paul said, looking in the rear-view mirror.

Paul stopped. The pickup's back-up lights came on and the vehicle backed up.

"Where get dog?" the driver said looking at Sandy.

"We found her in the ditch. Some asshole shot her," Anton said.

"Your dog?"

"She is now," Paul said.

"You go on farm?"

"No we haven't been on your farm. We found the dog injured. Not that it's any business of yours."

"You no go on farm. Posted."

"Listen pal, you stay on your side of the fence and we'll stay on ours," Anton said.

"Keep dog out too. We shoot if we see."

"Oh yeah?"

Anton started to get out of the Mule.

"Anton, no!"

The kid stopped. He was angry.

"You shoot at any dogs we know and we'll call the sheriff," Paul said.

The two Mexican guys looked uneasy at the mention of the sheriff.

"Just keep out," the passenger said.

"Up yours," Anton said.

They sat there for half a minute and then they drove off.

"Up yours?" Paul said grinning.

Anton laughed.

"I might have been a bit brash. They look like they're pretty tough, but I was so dang angry knowing they shot poor Sandy. I guess I should have re-thought that idea of getting out of the Mule."

"At least you listened to me."

"At least I had the good sense to do that. Let's go home. I want to do some jumps."

Paul ruffled his new brother's hair and they turned into their driveway. He sure didn't have to worry about not being backed up if he ever got into a scrape with this kid along.

Chapter 40

The boys cut wood and hauled it down to the house for the next two days. They had a huge pile of big thick logs that needed to be split so they drove to town and went to the garden center to see about a wood splitter.

There were three of them in different sizes. The guy from the garden center asked them how big their wood was and he suggested the middle-sized machine. He showed them how to use it and they filled out the rental form and hooked it to the back of the Mule.

Of course they had to stop for lunch and today they went to KFC so they could get some chicken nuggets for the dogs.

"Once we get that wood split and stacked we'll have enough for two years," Paul said.

"That should make Dad happy," Anton added.

"What are we gonna do to keep from getting bored now?"

"We can ride the dirt bike and maybe figure out a way to spy on the Mexicans."

Paul grinned at his brother.

"You're going to get us into trouble," he said.

"We won't go over the fence. I was thinking that if we went up on the hill we might be able to see down into the valley and see what they're doing."

"We'll see. For now let's worry about all of that wood and get it taken care of."

They went home and set up the splitter by the pile of big

logs. They laid a chunk of wood on the splitter and pulled the handle and the pneumatic ram pushed it against a wedge-shaped steel post and the thing split apart like it was made of soft butter.

"Oh this is going to be a snap," Anton said.

They took turns hauling the wood to the splitter and after a half hour they had a quite a pile of split wood on the ground. They took a time-out from splitting and stacked the wood. Then they took a break.

"Let's drive the Mule up on the hill and look around," Anton said.

"You're bound and determined to get a look into that farm aren't you?"

Anton shrugged.

"I'm a curious boy."

They followed an old logging road up the hill as far as they could go on it. When they got three quarters of the way up there was a big tree across the road and there was no way around it, even in the sure-footed Mule.

"Let's hike up," Anton said.

"Against my better judgment, okay," Paul said.

They made the dogs stay right with them. They weren't sure if they could get under the fence and didn't want to let them wander off. The hill was steep and it took some doing to get up to the top.

There was too much brush to see into the next valley.

"Crap, we can't see anything," Anton said.

Paul looked up into the trees around them.

"I wonder if one of us could climb up there and see?"

"Boost me up," Anton said.

Paul made a foot hold in his hands and Anton got up onto the lower branches of a big oak. He climbed slowly and steadily up until he was a long way off the ground.

Patrick sat and looked up and then he looked at Paul with a

very concerned look on his face.

"He's okay," Paul assured the dog.

Up in the tree Anton found he could see down into the valley on the other side of the fence, but he couldn't see the whole valley.

"I can see an old house that's all fallen down," he said looking down at Paul. "It was falling down when I was up here two years ago. They're not living in the house, that's for sure."

"Better come down. They might see you up there and pick you off like a squirrel."

Anton grinned and climbed down the tree.

"Well there's a kind of a camp and it looks like some building up the hill a little ways. I don't see any corn growing or anything like that."

"I doubt if corn is on their list of crops," Paul said.

"Man, I sure wish we could see what they're up to," Anton said shaking his head.

Chapter 41

The next morning they were eating breakfast and the TV was on. There was a story on about how the guy who founded Amazon was working on a system of little drones to deliver packages. Anton heard them talking and went to the living room to watch.

"Paul come here," he said.

Paul carried his cereal bowl in and sat and watched the story. It showed a little machine with a four propellers on it that flew with a remote control. The guy doing the story related that eventually Amazon would have a fleet of these little drones to deliver small items with in hours of them being ordered.

"That's what we need," Anton said.

"What, one of those drones?"

"Yeah, we can tape a camera on it and see what those guys are doing in the valley."

"That one on the news story was probably the only one of them there is. It was probably a prototype."

"I'm going to look."

Anton booted up his laptop and soon he was on Amazon. He typed in drone and a page came up with dozens of them on it.

"Holy smokes! Look at this!"

Paul looked and there were many different styles of drones

and many different prices for them. They found one that was exactly like the one on the TV show.

"Look at this one," Anton said. He clicked on the drone and a window opened.

"This one has a video camera on it."

He read the description.

"You can have the video feed transmitted to a laptop. Paul this is what we need!"

"How much is it?"

"It's about a hundred bucks."

"It that all? Are you sure these aren't just toys?"

"Well they say they're the real thing."

Paul thought about it. It would be fun to fly over the farm and watch it on their laptop.

"You know we've hauled a butt-load of firewood. I wonder if Mom and Dad would let us have one?"

Anton grinned.

"They should. Of course we wouldn't want to tell them we wanted it so we could spy on the Mexicans."

"Oh heck no. But if we suggested it as an educational tool, we might get it."

"You're devious" Anton said.

Paul grinned.

"I'm curious like you. I wonder how loud they are?"

"That one on the TV program didn't make much noise."

He clicked on YouTube and found hundreds of videos of the drones. They watched several of them.

"Where have we been? These things are everywhere."

"We've been cutting too much firewood," Paul said.

"So, do you think we can try for one?"

"Print that page," Paul said.

"And they're going to use them to deliver packages," Paul was saying at the dinner table.

"What do you two want with one?"

"They'd be fun to play with. We can fly it over the farm and learn about aviation and stuff," Anton said.

"They're something that will be very common in the future. Who knows, one of us might be a drone driver someday," Paul added.

"How much are they?"

"Well they run from about forty bucks to three hundred. The one we like is about a hundred bucks."

"They have cut a lot of firewood Honey," their mom said.

"True. Okay use our card and order it. But as usual, it's a parent's duty to say, 'be careful with it.'"

"We will."

They ran to their room and Anton woke up his computer. It was on the page he wanted already. All he had to do was click a couple of buttons.

Chapter 42

They were waiting as the UPS truck drove into the driveway. Every day for the last three days they had waited and been disappointed when the UPS truck went right past their driveway. Today was different.

They ran out to the truck and Paul signed for the package. They ran to the house and to their room and tore it open.

"Holy cow it's in a million pieces!"

"Wow, there aren't a million pieces but there are a hundred or more," Paul said.

They dumped out all of the pieces on the table and got the instructions out. The instructions were complicated and there were thirty pages of them.

"Oh man, I was hoping to be flying it by now," Anton said.

"Well we've got to take our time and do this right or we'll never get it off the ground."

They started with the first instruction and took their time and slowly but surely the thing came together. Once they'd built one of the four motors the other three were pretty easy to build. Then the put it all together and added the controls and the camera.

"We have to charge the battery before we can test it," Anton said. They put the battery in a charger and turned to the instructions for making the pictures from the camera show up on a laptop.

There was a disk and they followed the instructions and set up the program on Paul's laptop. Then they plugged in the remote control unit to charge.

"No wonder they cost less than we expected," Anton said.

"Yeah, the labor they save by dumping all that stuff in a box is worth an extra hundred bucks."

It was maddening waiting for everything to charge up but finally both units were charged and ready to go. They took the drone out to the middle of the yard and Paul sat it in the grass.

They stood a little way away and Anton clicked the on button. The four propellers began turning slowly.

"Holy smokes, it works," he said.

"Try to lift off."

Anton used the controls and gave the drone more power. The thing shakily lifted from the ground and hovered a foot off the grass. Patrick ran toward it.

"Patrick no!"

The dog stopped and looked at the thing and then backed off.

"That'd be great. We just get it flying and Patrick smashes it to pieces."

Anton worked the joystick and soon the drone moved to the right. Then he moved it back to the left.

He moved the stick to increase the altitude and the thing went up to about ten feet off the ground.

"Don't go any higher until we figure out how to run it. That way if we crash it won't be ruined."

Anton worked on the drone and soon he had it flying back and forth across the grass. He made it dive toward the dogs and they took off running for their lives.

"Here try it," he said handing the control unit to Paul.

Paul was a little shaky at first but soon he got the thing running pretty well. He pushed the switch for the camera and they saw the ground appear on the laptop. He turned the control and the camera panned to the left and there they were looking up at the thing.

"Wow it works great," Paul said.

They took turns running the thing and it was a very cool

toy. They flew it higher and soon they were looking down from fifty feet over the ground. Anton flew it out over the creek and they could easily see everything below the drone.

"We could see everything they're doing up in that valley," Paul said.

"Here, take over. I'm going to run down there below it and see how much noise it makes," Anton said.

Paul flew the drone and Anton ran down into the valley. Paul flew it right over him and he heard a slight buzz but nothing very loud. It sounded more like an insect than something mechanical.

By the time Anton got back by Paul he was flying the thing back towards them.

"The power dial says we're getting low on battery," Paul said.

"How long have we been playing with it?"

"I'd guess half an hour to three quarters of an hour."

"Good to know."

Paul landed the drone on the grass. They turned to each other and bumped fists.

"This is going to be amazing," Paul said.

"No foolin."

They took it to their bedroom and plugged both units in to be charged.

"I wonder how far away it can get from the control unit?" Anton asked.

"We better find out tomorrow so we don't lose it."

"Good idea. It wouldn't be good for it to drop into the Mexican's camp."

"You can buy extra battery packs for the drone. I think we should get one so we have longer time to fly it," Anton said.

He went online and ordered a second battery pack. They'd charge it up and that way they'd always have twice as much flying time.

Chapter 43

The boys drove up to the pond the next morning. They planned on flying the drone and spending the day fishing and just relaxing. Paul drove the Mule up and Anton rode his bike. The dogs rode with Paul.

They flew the drone up and around the pond and were amazed at how much they could see with the camera on it. Anton flew it up over the hill where the trees were all blown down and it was pretty amazing to see how much wood there was.

"We can cut firewood until we're old men and never run out," Paul said.

"Yippee."

They both laughed.

"Actually I kind of like making wood. It's not a bad job and when I think of how nice and warm it will make the house next winter I think it's worth it."

"The drone is getting low on battery," Anton said.

"Let's go back and charge it and make some sandwiches and then come back up and fish for a while," Paul said.

That's what they did. Anton plugged the battery into the charger and they made sandwiches and got a new block of ice from the freezer for their cooler at the tent. It only took a half hour to charge the battery and they were on their way back. They parked the Mule and zipped the tent open.

"Didn't we put our fishing poles in here?" Anton asked.

"Yeah, I'm sure we did," Paul said.

"Well they're not here now."

They looked carefully under the sleeping bags and the poles weren't in the tent. Paul walked down by the pond and looked to be sure they had picked them up and they weren't anywhere to be seen.

"Our cooler is gone too," Anton said.

"No lie?"

"Somebody's been here and stole our crap."

They both looked up the valley toward the Mexican's land.

"I bet those turds came down here and helped themselves," Paul said.

"What are we going to do?"

"Do you think they'd hear the drone if you flew it up there?" Paul asked.

"If I keep it pretty high I don't think so. It's breezy today so there'd be some wind and noise. Should we try it?"

"Let's."

They walked up to the fence at the bottom of the valley.

"I'm not sure how far I can fly it before I loose control with the remote," Anton said.

"Well let's take it slow and see."

Anton hit the power button and the drone lifted off the ground. He flew it up about twenty feet in the air and then started it going up the valley. They watched the laptop and could see the ground going past on the screen. There wasn't much to see but trees and brush.

"What was that?"

Anton slowed the drone and turned it so it went back to where it had been. A pump sat next to the stream and a power cord looked like it ran up the hill.

"That's where they're pumping water," Paul said.

"Let's see where the cord goes."

Anton followed the cord up the hill. Soon they saw a pile of food cans that had been opened and were empty. Then they found a pile of other garbage and a shabby tent. There were clothes strung from a rope tied between two trees and a couple of camp chairs and a pile of ashes where they'd had a campfire.

"Nice place," Anton said.

"Look there," Paul said pointing to the edge of the screen.

"Our cooler!"

Sure enough, their cooler was sitting next to a tree.

"See what's up the valley farther," Paul said.

Anton flew the drone up into the valley. The floor of the valley leveled out and there were rows of trees planted on the flat ground.

"What are those?"

"They look like Christmas trees."

"No way. Those are pot plants."

"They're huge. They can't be pot plants can they?" Paul said.

"Well I've never seen a Christmas tree that looked like that with long pointed leaves."

Just then their drone began to move off to the left. Anton tried to move it back.

"Uh oh, the battery is almost dead. I didn't watch it."

"Get it back," Paul said.

Anton turned the drone and headed it back toward them. It flew on but it was slowing down.

"I'm losing altitude," he said.

"How far is it away?"

Anton listened.

"I can hear it."

He looked in the air and Paul watched the screen of the laptop.

"It's getting lower," he said, "It's almost in the trees."

"Oh man the battery says zero power."

"It's coming down!"

They both looked at the screen and the camera got closer and closer to a big bush. Suddenly all they could see was leaves and then dirt.

"It crashed!" Anton said.

Chapter 44

"**W**hat are we going to do now?" Paul asked.
"We have to go get it."
"Anton they have guns."
"We didn't see any of them. Maybe they're in town. The drone landed just a little way inside the fence. I could hear it."

"Oh man, I don't think this is a good idea."

"What are we going to say if Mom and Dad ask us where the drone is?"

Paul had no answer.

"We can't tell them it's in the valley and we were spying on the Mexicans."

"Oh boy, I don't like this."

"Listen, I'll go under the fence by the creek. It's loose there and I can get under. Let me get in there a little way and then turn the switch to ON. There is probably a little bit of power left. It will let the rotors spin a few times. I should be able to hear it and then I'll grab it and be out of there like a flash."

"Anton let's just tell Mom and Dad it got away from us and landed up there. They'll be okay about it."

"No way. They'll know we were snooping and our drone will be gone forever. Come on Paul, I'm quick. I promise I'll be in and out in no time."

Against his better judgment, Paul agreed. He looked at Anton and the kid was wearing a bright red shirt.

"We have to run down to the house and you need to change into something that isn't so easy to see," Paul said.

They got in the Mule and hurried to the house. Anton went in and put on a dark green shirt and then they drove back up to the fence. They walked up to where the stream ran through the fence. Where the land dropped low beside the stream there was a gap between the fence and the ground.

"Give me a couple of minutes to get up there. Then switch it on and off a couple of times and I should be able to hear it."

"Okay but if you see any of those guys, get the heck out of there."

Anton nodded and slithered under the fence. He climbed up out of the stream ditch and began working his way through the dense brush.

It was slow going. There were a lot of willows and they were very close together making it hard to move though them. Once he got up in the valley a little way it cleared out a little. He worked to the left side of the valley where he'd heard the drone last.

He knew he was in the general area so he stopped and waited for Paul to switch the rotors on. Suddenly he heard a whirring sound ahead of him. He started for the sound.

"What is noise?"

He stopped. One of the Mexicans spoke up in front of him. He must have heard the rotors too.

"Hear nada."

There were two of them.

Paul turned on the rotors again.

"Hear?"

"Si."

"I have to get it quick," Anton said.

He began moving through the brush as fast as he could without making a lot of noise. Suddenly he heard someone coming through the brush behind him.

"Oh crap," he thought. "They found me."

He turned and here came Patrick running toward him.

"Patrick!" he whispered.

The dog ran to him wagging his tail.

"What the heck? Sit!"

The dog sat.

"Stay here."

Patrick sat and wagged his tail. Anton moved forward and then he saw the drone hung in a bush. He quickly pulled it from the branches and hurried back to Patrick.

"Come on," he said.

"Someone here," the voice said.

"Stop or shoot!"

Anton was almost running now. He went crashing through the brush and didn't worry about the noise. He had to get under the fence!

Suddenly there were two shots fired. He stopped but then took off running again. He ran right into the fence. Then he turned and ran down the fence to the stream and shinnied under. Patrick was right behind him.

"Holy crap, are you okay?" Paul asked.

"I think so," he said looking at his body for blood. "Does Patrick have any holes in him?"

Paul looked the dog over.

"He's fine. Let's get out of here."

They ran toward the pond. Once they got there they felt pretty safe. The Mexicans might be brave enough to raid their camp in the dark but probably wouldn't bother them in the daylight.

"Jeez, I almost had a heart attack when I heard those shots," Paul said.

"You! I almost peed my pants. I think they heard me and were just shooting to scare me."

"Well they succeeded."

"No fooling."

Paul picked up the drone.

"It looks okay," he said.

"It didn't even hit the ground. It was in a bush."

"Well so much for that idea."

"What are we going to do? We know they're growing pot in there."

"But we can't do anything about it. If we tell the sheriff, Mom and Dad will know we messed with those guys despite their strict orders not to."

"We've got to think about what to do. We can't just let them get away with it. And besides they stole our stuff too."

"Come on, let's go home. We'll think about it over night," Paul said.

Chapter 45

T he boys charged up the drone and the laptop. They decided to sleep in the tent so they packed some pop and snacks in another cooler and drove the Mule up to the pond.

"I think I can record the video onto my hard drive," Anton said. "Then we can download it onto a flash drive."

"If we get some good pictures of the pot field we can drop if off anonymously at the Sheriff's office," Paul said.

"Yup. Then goodbye Mexican drug guys."

They sat by the fire pit and talked. The dogs lay next to their masters and snoozed. Up in the valley they heard a shot.

"I wonder what they shoot at?" Paul said.

"Who knows? Maybe they just like to shoot."

It was still nearly eighty degrees when it turned dark. Just after dark they began to see lightning in the west.

"Looks like it's going to storm," Paul said.

"Yeah," Anton said quietly.

"It'll be okay."

"I know. I just think back to that other storm and it was just like this."

"Storms are common when it's hot and humid like it was today. If you're uncomfortable we can go home," Paul said.

"No I've got to get over the fear of storms and if I run and hide every time it thunders I'll never do it."

They watched the storm approaching. An hour later the

whole horizon was aglow with lightning. Then it started to sprinkle.

They went inside and zipped up the tent. The rain increased and soon it was pounding on the fabric of the tent.

"I hope this thing doesn't leak," Paul said shining his shaker light up to the top of the ceiling.

"Don't touch it. I've heard if you touch a wet tent it'll leak."

"Don't worry I won't."

The rain continued and the storm got closer. Now when the lightning flashed the thunder was almost immediate.

"It's almost here," Paul said.

Then suddenly the rain stopped. The thunder and lightning increased and it was deadly calm.

Anton zipped one of the window open facing west.

"It's so calm. What's going on?"

"I'm not sure. I think we should have gone to the house," Paul said.

"Turn the radio on," Anton said.

Paul turned the little radio on and there was a lot of static and an announcer warning of a tornado touchdown. He went on and on and finally said it had touched down on the highway west of their farm.

"That's not far," Paul said.

"Oh man, we gotta go!" Anton said.

"Listen!"

They heard it. It was the sound they'd been told that people heard when a tornado was approaching, the sound of a freight train.

"It's coming!"

"We'll never make it home!"

Anton was shaking. He was terrified. He knew what a tornado could do.

"The cave!" Paul shouted.

"Run for it."

They zipped the tent open. They each took a flashlight and ran for the hill. The dogs were right behind them.

"It's coming!"

Paul looked over his shoulder and he could see the funnel coming over the south end of the valley. It was going right over the path of downed trees that the last one had torn to pieces.

"Hurry!"

They ran up the hill as fast as they could. The trees were whipping back and forth and sticks and leaves were flying through the air.

"Up there!"

Paul shined his light on the entrance to the cave. They climbed as fast as they could. The dogs were terrified and stuck right to them. Paul got to the cave first and crawled inside. He called Sandy and she went in and then Patrick hurried in too.

"Come on, hurry!" he said.

Anton was so out of breath he could hardly put one foot in front of the other. The ground was wet and his feet slid out from under him and he skidded down the hill in the mud. He got up and climbed back up but he was exhausted. He staggered and fell. A big branch fell off the tree above them and landed on top of him. Paul told the dogs to wait and ran down the hill to Anton and pulled the branch off him. He picked his brother up and dragged him into the cave.

Dirt and debris was flying in the opening so they moved back into the cave a few feet.

"Hang onto the dogs," Anton said clutching Patrick tightly.

The howl of the wind was deafening. There was garbage flying into the cave so they moved deeper inside.

"We're okay, there's no way it can hurt us in here," Paul said.

He'd no more than said those words when there came a thunderous crash. The ground shook and the ceiling of the cave collapsed. Dirt and dust billowed up around them so they couldn't see each other.

They pulled their tee shirts up over their noses so they could breathe.

"What the heck was that?" Anton asked.

Paul shined his light toward the entrance to the cave. The entrance was gone. All they could see was a huge pile of dirt and rocks and some roots hanging down from the top of the pile.

"One of those big trees must have blown over and it landed on top of the entrance."

"Oh no. We're trapped."

Chapter 46

The boys sat and looked around them. The dust was settling so their vision was improving.

"It sounds like there's still a lot of thunder," Paul said.

"We're safe in here at least," Anton added.

"I think we should just wait it out. We won't do ourselves any good digging out and finding the storm still raging."

Anton agreed so they each huddled with his dog and settled back against the cave wall. They left their flashlights on.

It was totally dark when Anton woke. At first he didn't know where he was. Then Patrick licked his face and he remembered they were in the cave. He felt around and found one of the flashlights and shook it hard. The shaker charged the battery and the light shined out over the cave. Paul woke.

"We fell asleep," he said yawning.

"Yeah, it sounds pretty quiet out there."

Paul charged his flashlight. He shined it at the pile of rubble.

"Wow, I don't think we're going to get out through that. Look at all the rocks and dirt."

They crawled over to the pile and looked it over. It filled the cave from side to side and all the way up to the top.

"We're going to have to go out the top entrance," Anton said.

"And come out behind the fence."

"What if that end is closed up too?"

"The chances of both ends getting closed are a million to one," Paul said.

"You said the chances of another tornado coming down this

174

valley were a million to one too," Anton said.

"Well, I guess I was wrong about that."

"At least we got out of the tent. I flew through the air once, I sure as heck didn't want to do that again."

"We'll have to take our chances that the other end is open. We really don't have much choice," Paul said.

Paul took the lead and they started up the tunnel. The dogs trotted along with them. They walked in some parts and crawled in others. They came to a split.

"The last time we came in here we took the right tunnel," Paul said.

"I remember," Anton answered and they went down the tunnel to the right.

They stooped over and crawled in some places. The dogs hurried ahead of them and they had to keep calling them back so they didn't go out and get seen by their neighbors.

"The other split," Anton said.

"Right again," Paul said.

They started down the tunnel and it got very small. They had to get down on their bellies and shinny though. They crawled for at least fifty feet and then they came to the end but there were tree branches blocking their way out.

"The wind blew a lot of stuff into this hole too," Paul said.

Anton was in the front and there wasn't room for both of them, so he began working his way into the branches. His head popped out of the pile and he stood up. He got his shoulders out of the mess and began tossing branches off to the side to open the hole. He climbed out and Paul and the dogs followed.

It was still dark. They crouched by the hole and listened.

"They must be sleeping." Paul said.

"We might not be anywhere near them," Anton suggested.

"True. I think we should just sit and wait for it to get light so we can figure out where we are."

"Good idea," Anton said. He whispered to Patrick and he

175

and the dog lay down in a pile of the soft branches. Paul and Sandy did the same. It didn't take long for them to fall asleep.

Paul woke when he smelled the smoke. He looked around and poked Anton with a stick. He held up his finger to his lips telling him to be quiet.

"I smell a campfire," he whispered.

Anton nodded.

They got up and crawled through the brush carefully. Each of them had to keep their dog close and tried to keep them quiet.

They heard laughter below them in the valley.

"We're right above them," Paul said.

"We must be inside the fence," Anton whispered.

Paul nodded.

He looked around.

"I think we need to go this way," he said pointing to the right and downhill."

"Yeah, but we've got to be quiet."

They started creeping through the brush. It was thick and it was slow going. They could hear the Mexicans talking below them.

The dogs were excited and they had to keep telling them to stay and tried to keep them quiet.

They came to a very thick area of brush. There was a small trail through it like something a deer might make. They started crawling down the trail.

"I hope this goes all the way to the bottom," Paul whispered.

They were nearly through the thicket when they heard something move ahead of them. They stopped.

Suddenly a grouse took off and made a heck of a racket with its wings as it rose up through the brush. Patrick saw it and ran after it howling.

"Oh no!" Anton said.

Chapter 47

There was excited chatter coming from the camp below them. They heard the sound of more than one person moving through the brush toward them.

"Who there?"

Two shots rang out.

Patrick came running back to Anton with his tail between his legs. Sandy cowered.

"Be still," Paul whispered.

"Come out or we shoot."

"Hold onto the dogs and stay here," Paul whispered.

"What? What are you going to do?"

"Stay put until they're gone."

Paul got to his feet and ran down the hill through the brush. He crashed into trees and plowed through brush until he was fifty feet from Anton and the dogs. The Mexicans ran after him shouting.

When he was far enough he stopped and raised his hands.

"Don't shoot. I give up."

The Mexicans gathered around him with their guns pointed at him. They were all jabbering Spanish and Paul had no idea what they were saying.

Eventually one who seemed to be the leader stepped up to him. He looked really angry.

"What you do here?"

"The storm came while I was camping and I ran trying to get away from it. I must have strayed into your land. I'm sorry

I'll leave."

The guy slapped him hard.

"You no go anywhere."

Paul picked himself up off the ground. His nose was bleeding. He wiped the blood off his face.

"It was an accident. I didn't mean to come here."

"Where is dog?"

"The dog ran off chasing a bird. A grouse."

"What grouse?"

"A bird, like a chicken."

The guy seemed to know what he meant.

"Where other boy?"

"He is home. He was sick. Didn't want to camp."

The guy thought it over.

"You come with us."

"Okay, just watch those guns," Paul said. Then he said loudly, "I'll go to your camp with you."

Anton stayed perfectly still. He heard the guys moving through the brush away from him. He could hear them talking Spanish as they got farther away.

"Come with me," he whispered to the dogs.

They were both pretty scared so he didn't think they'd run off. They followed right alongside him and he snuck down the trail and worked his way through the brush to the bottom of the hill. He crawled down into the ditch where the stream ran and they followed the ditch to the valley. He and the dogs crawled under the fence.

"Oh man, we gotta get home and tell Dad and Mom."

He ran down the valley to the pond. The Mule was there and although it had a lot of branches and junk on it, it looked like it wasn't hurt. He cleared the stuff off and started it.

The dogs jumped up onto the back and he roared off toward the farm.

"I hope the house is still there," he though as he drove

THE BOY WHO FELL FROM THE SKY

dodging debris that was scattered over the ground.

When he got close enough he could see the house. It looked like it had some siding missing and a few shingles but it was standing. He saw his dad coming out of the house when he heard the Mule.

"Where's Paul?"

"He's okay but the Mexicans got him."

"The Mexicans? What were you doing up there?"

"The tornado was coming. We knew we couldn't get back here so we ran up to the cave and hid in it. A big tree fell on it and caved in the entrance. We had to follow it to the other end and it came out on the wrong side of the fence. They heard Patrick and Paul let them catch him so I could get away."

His mom was now on the porch with them.

"We've been nearly insane with worry. We saw the tent flattened but had no idea where you guys were," she said hugging him.

"Call the Sheriff," Anton said.

"The cell tower must have been damaged or blown down. There's no phone service."

"We'll have to drive into town and go to the Sheriff," his dad said.

"I'll stay here in case Paul gets away," Anton said.

"You be sure to stay right here," his mom said.

"I will."

The parents got in one of the cars and drove off. Anton watched them go and then he ran into their room. He grabbed the extra battery pack and then he dug in his dresser drawer and grabbed a few things. Then he and the dogs jumped into the Mule and headed up to the pond.

"We can't wait for the Sheriff," he said to the dogs.

Chapter 48

Anton drove the Mule as fast as he dared with the dogs in the back. He got to the pond and found the tent was flattened but still there. The poles had collapsed but the fabric still was fastened to the ground with the tent pegs.

There was a lot of debris everywhere so he had to clear it away so he could find the door. He finally found it and zipped it open. The dogs were running around checking things out so he crawled inside and began looking for the drone. It was upside down but it looked like it would work. He found the control unit and the antenna was bent but it also looked like it was in working condition. He grabbed both and crawled out of the tent.

"I better check it out before I go up to the valley," he thought.

He sat the drone on the grass and hit the power button. The propellers began rotating. He worked the joystick and it lifted off.

"Good," he said.

He found the backpack that they'd carried the control box and the laptop in and the laptop was there and seemed ready to go.

He knew the dogs wouldn't stay behind so he started for the valley on foot. He didn't want to take the Mule up in case someone was close by and they would hear him coming.

He was a quarter of the way up to the valley when he stopped. He sat the drone on the ground and ran back to the tent. He crawled inside again and rummaged around all of the blankets and sleeping bags. He found the big zip lock bag that held their fireworks. He looked through the plastic and saw the lighter they'd used to fire a few of them off one night.

He ran back and picked up the drone and then hurried up to the fence at the bottom of the valley.

There was a stump near the fence to he sat the laptop on it and powered it up. Then he powered up the drone and the camera. Everything was working.

"Okay, here we go," he said. The dogs wagged their tails.

The drone lifted off and he flew it up to around thirty feet up in the air. He steered it up the valley, and aimed the camera down so he could see what was below him.

"Their camp is on the right side of the valley," he said. "That's probably where they have Paul."

The drone flew on and he panned the camera back and forth looking for any of the drug guys. There was no one under it.

Then he got to where he could see their tent and their garbage. He hovered over that spot and zoomed down looking for Paul.

"Maybe they took him someplace else," he thought.

He found the old house and it was flat. It had blown down in the storm. Then he saw Paul's feet sticking out from the side of a tree. He moved the drone and then he could see him. His hands were tied behind him and he was tied to the tree. He looked up when he heard the drone.

Anton made the drone wiggle from side to side. Paul shook his head.

"Don't tell me not to come. That's not going to work."

He flew the drone up the valley farther looking for the drug guys. When he got to the pot field it looked different. The rows of big plants were gone and most of the plants were lying in piles. Then he saw the guys at the far end. They were using machetes and chopping the plants down.

"They must be going to harvest them and then get out of here," he said.

He turned the drone around and headed it back down the valley. A red light began blinking.

"Oh no, low battery already?"

The drone was getting low on power. He had to get it back quickly or it would fall out of the sky. He flew it directly toward the fence. The power bar was down to one bar.

"Oh boy," he though.

Then he heard the drone. He looked up and it was thirty feet inside the fence. It was coming but it was dropping too. He tried to hurry it and it just cleared the fence when the rotors stopped turning and it fell from the sky.

He shut it down and turned off the laptop.

He picked up the backpack and the fireworks and dumped them into the backpack.

"You guys stay! Stay!"

The dogs sat down.

Anton crawled under the fence and started up the ditch of the stream.

Chapter 49

He stayed in the bottom of the creek bed as much as he could. That way he could step from stone to stone and not take the chance of snapping a twig or crunching dead leaves.

He made pretty good progress. He stopped for a breather and to look ahead to see where to go next when he heard something move in the brush. He crouched down.

His heart was beating like a jackhammer. If one of the pot growers was there they might shoot first and ask questions later.

He heard the sound again. He flattened himself against the ground. The sound came closer. He looked up. Patrick was standing there wagging his tail. Sandy was right behind him.

"I told you guys to stay!" he said.

The dogs swarmed him licking his hands and face.

"Dang, well you have to be quiet," he said.

He started out again. The dogs saw him sneaking and they seemed to get the idea. They both walked quietly and stayed behind him.

He moved up the valley for another ten minutes. He knew he must be close to the camp so he started up the left side of the creek bank. Now he had to move very slowly so he didn't make any noise.

Suddenly he smelled smoke. The campfire at the camp must have been close. He moved forward and he could see the orange tent through the brush.

"Shhh," he shushed the dogs.

They crept forward. He didn't see any movement. The fire

pit was smoldering so it looked like they had all left to harvest the pot.

He crawled on his hands and knees. Then he looked where he'd seen Paul and he could see his feet sticking out from behind the tree. He crawled over near him. Suddenly Paul looked around the tree.

"What the heck are you doing?" he whispered.

"I'm rescuing you."

"You're going to get us shot."

"They're up in the valley harvesting the pot."

"Is that where they went? I heard them jabbering in Spanish. I didn't know what they were talking about but they were pretty excited."

While they were talking Anton took the backpack off and dug in it and came out with his jack knife. He cut the ropes on the tree letting Paul loose and then he cut his hands free.

"They probably figured since they took you captive they had to get out of here. I bet they're going to cut the pot and then get in here and haul it out."

"We gotta tell the Sheriff.'

"Mom and Dad went to get him. The cell phone tower must have been blown down in the tornado."

"Do they know you came up here?"

"Of course not."

Paul shook his head.

"Do you have some kind of plan?"

"Well I was kind of making it up as I went," Anton said.

"What else do you have with you?"

"I've got the fireworks."

"No move!"

The voice came from behind them. They both turned and looked.

One of the Mexicans was standing behind them carrying an empty water jug. He had a pistol in his other hand.

"Oh crap," Paul said.

The guy sat the jug down. He moved toward them.

"Put hands behind back."

Suddenly there was a low growling sound. The guy started to turn toward it. There was a blur of tan hair as Sandy leapt from the bushes and clamped her teeth onto the guy's wrist. He began screaming and dropped the gun. Sandy's momentum made him loose his balance and he fell over. When he hit the ground Patrick leapt on top of him and grabbed the front of his shirt and began growling and shaking his head.

"Get the gun!" Paul shouted.

Anton dove on top of the gun and grabbed it. He stood up holding it with both hands. His hands were shaking.

"Sandy, come here!" Paul said.

"Patrick," Anton said.

The two dogs let loose of the guy and came to them.

"Don't freakin' move!" Anton warned. "I'm not a very good shot and I might just shoot your balls off!"

Chapter 50

Anton's hands were shaking. He held the gun on the guy but had no idea if it was on safety or not.

Paul stepped up to him.

"Let me have it," he said.

Anton handed him the gun. Paul checked and the safety was off. The gun was ready to fire.

"Amigos coming. You in trouble," the guy said.

"Shut up. It won't do you any good if they come and find you with a hole in your dick," Paul said aiming at the guy's crotch.

He stepped back keeping the gun trained on the guy.

"Okay we have to think this out. I doubt the others are coming. I think this guy just came for water so we have a few minutes to get out of here."

"Do you think we can make it before they catch up to us?" Anton asked.

"We can if they think the law is here."

Anton looked at Paul and grinned. He had a plan.

They tied the drug guy to a tree and Paul found an old shirt and tore a piece of out and they gagged him so he couldn't yell. They looked around the camp and found a toolbox. Paul dug through it and found a wire cutter.

"We need a diversion," Anton said.

"Okay I'm listening."

"I'll sneak up above those guys who are cutting the pot and set off a bunch of cherry bombs and yell that I'm the cops. That should make them take off up the valley. Then we can go like a bunny and get down to the fence and onto our farm. Hopefully the Sheriff will be here by then."

"It's a good plan except for the part where you sneak up there. I don't like that idea."

"We have to get them farther away so we have time to get out of here."

"It's too risky."

"Look, we're wasting time while we talk. They'll come looking for this guy if he doesn't get back pretty soon."

Paul picked up the backpack. He dumped out the fireworks.

"You brought the roman candles too. We can shoot them up into the valley from here. That will spook them and give us time to get out."

"Okay, I think the cherry bombs would be better but I'm good with that."

They pulled a tent stake out of the ground and then snuck up onto the hillside where it was clear of brush. Paul poked the tent stake into the ground and made a hole for one of the roman candles and Anton shoved it in. They made ten holes all together and filled each with a roman candle.

"Okay, you gather up the dogs and start for the fence. I'll give you a minute and then light these and be right behind you," Paul said.

"I can set them off."

"No you get the dogs and get going. Don't worry I won't be far behind. Take that wire cutter and make the hole bigger so I can slide through."

Anton agreed and he quietly called the dogs. They set off back towards the camp. He hurried but tried not to make too much noise.

Paul waited. He could hear the other guys talking in the valley. It was obvious they'd been cutting the pot for a few days because most of it was not visible from the hillside.

"If the Sheriff gets here in time they can catch them and grab all that pot and destroy it," he thought.

Anton came to the camp. He stopped and his heart began

beating quickly. The drug guy was gone!

"Oh boy."

He stood there for a second. If the guy went back and told his pals they'd get Paul. If not he must be...

The guy came out of nowhere. He grabbed Anton by the neck and threw him to the ground. Anton landed on his side and heard something in his shoulder snap. The guy slapped him in the face and grabbed him around the throat. He began choking him. Anton couldn't breathe and he started seeing stars. He didn't want to die in this drug camp.

"Paul!" Anton yelled as loud as he could but with the guy's hands around his throat it wasn't very loud. He tried to kick to get the guy off him but he was too strong.

"Oh no, he's going to strangle me," he thought.

His ears began ringing. He could see the guy but his vision was getting blurry.

"Help me," he whispered.

Suddenly he could breathe. He heard a heck of a loud battle going on. He tried to sit up but was too weak. He looked around and saw Sandy and Patrick on top of the guy and they were going at him like a pack of wolves. He was yelling in Spanish.

Anton tried to get up. He heard a lot of loud banging and looked up and saw bright streaks of light going across the sky. Maybe he was dead after all.

"Sandy! Patrick! Let go!"

He looked and there was Paul running toward them with a thick stick. The dogs jumped off the guy and Paul hit him with the club like he was hitting a home run. The club got the guy on the side of his head and he dropped like a stone.

"Are you okay?"

Anton grinned. "I am now."

Chapter 51

Paul reached down and helped Anton to his feet.
Anton moved his shoulder and sharp pain shot through his arm.

"I think I broke my shoulder," he said.

'We gotta get out of here fast!" Paul said. "The fireworks scared them off for a little while but they're going to figure it out pretty soon that it was just fireworks and not the Sheriff. We better be out of here before they come back here."

They left the guy who Paul had hit lying where he fell. He was out cold. They hurried down to the bottom of the valley and worked their way along the top of the ditch of the stream. It was faster going on the bank rather than down in the ditch where there were rocks and logs blocking the route.

They stopped for a breather. Paul looked back and he saw a lot of smoke in the air.

"Something's on fire," he said.

"It looks like it's up in the top of the valley where the pot field was. Do you suppose they're burning it?"

"I don't know but we better get moving."

They moved as fast as they could down the valley. Every now and then they stopped and listened to see if they could hear anyone coming behind them but there was no sound.

They finally came to the fence. Paul lifted up the wire and Anton slid under. Then the dogs crawled through and Paul came behind them.

"The drone," Anton said.

Paul picked it up and Anton picked up the control unit with

his good arm.

"Let's see what's going on," he said.

"I thought it was dead," Paul said.

"I brought the extra battery pack."

"Can you drive it with one hand?"

"No you'll have to drive it," Anton said.

They sat the drone on the ground and Anton changed the battery and Paul powered it up and made it take off. Paul was a little shaky on the controls. He was still pretty upset at nearly getting shot, but soon he had the thing in the air and heading up the valley.

"Lot's of smoke up there," Anton said looking in the air.

"It looks like a forest fire," Paul said.

They watched the laptop and soon the smoke got very thick. Paul flew the drone higher so it was above the smoke. Suddenly they saw flames.

"Holy smokes, the pot field is on fire," Paul said.

Sure enough, the piles of cut pot plants were burning and the fire had spread to the live plants and was even up in the woods in some places.

"One of those Roman Candles must have landed in a pile of that dry pot."

"Holy smokes, those guys are gonna be mad at us," Anton said.

"We better get out of here."

Paul turned the drone and started flying it back towards them. Anton ran down to the pond and started up the Mule and drove it up to the fence. By the time he got there Paul had the drone on the ground. He coaxed the dogs into the back and jumped in to drive.

"Let's get out of here!"

They took off for home. Behind them the smoke was billowing out of the valley.

"I hope the Sheriff is on the way," Paul said.

"I hope the fire department is on the way too."

"How is your shoulder?" Paul asked as they hurried into the house.

"It hurts like heck. Something popped in it when that guy slammed me. It might be broken or maybe dislocated."

Anton tried to lift his arm and he grimaced in pain. Paul ran to their room and came back with an elastic bandage he's used on his knee when he'd twisted it. He wrapped it around Anton's chest and right arm to keep them stabilized.

"We need to get you to the doctor."

"Shouldn't we wait for Mom and Dad?"

Paul was about to answer when the front door burst open. Three of the drug guys came hurrying in with guns in their hands.

"Oh no," Paul said.

Chapter 52

"Give keys to truck!"

"What truck? We don't have a truck," Paul said.

"Little truck outside. Give keys."

They wanted the Mule. Obviously their own vehicle was in the fire or disabled some way.

"Okay, just be cool with those guns," Paul said.

He stepped in front of Anton and when he reached into his pocket for the keys he lifted his shirt. Anton looked and was surprised to see the pistol that the guy that had attacked him was sticking out of the back of Paul's jeans. He hadn't seen him pick it up.

"Just a minute, I have them here someplace," Paul said.

Anton reached out with his left hand and pulled the pistol from Paul's pants and dropped his hand next to his side.

Paul pulled the keys from his pocket. He held them out to the front guy.

"Here, take it and go."

The back two guys lowered their guns and the front guy stepped up to take the keys. He dropped his gun to his side and reached out to grab the keys and when he did Anton raised the gun and put it right in the middle of his forehead.

"Don't you move you shithead! One move and I'll blow your stupid brains all over the floor."

The guy just about crapped his pants. His eyes got big and he stopped and stood still like a statue.

"No shoot, we go."

"Tell your friends to throw their guns on the floor," Paul

said.

The guy rattled some Spanish and the other two tossed their guns onto the floor near Paul and Anton.

"Now you."

The head guy reached for his gun.

"Very slowly. One false move and you'll be very sorry for it."

He lifted the gun slowly and Paul grabbed it and held it on him."

"Okay, all three of you. Back out of the door."

The three of them backed out and onto the porch. Anton and Paul followed them with guns trained on them.

"On the ground, hands behind your backs," Paul said.

"Is this thing on safe or on go?" Anton whispered.

"It's on safe. Move that little lever."

Anton flicked the safety off with his thumb.

"I'm going to get a rope. If they move, blow their balls off."

"I'm not aiming for anyplace in particular. If they move, I'm just going to shoot until I don't have any bullets left."

The three guys looked at him and it was pretty plain to see, they believed him. Paul ran to the garage and came back with a length of rope. He tied one of the guy's hands and then the next and the next. They were all tied with the same rope.

"Okay, now we'll just wait for the Sheriff," Paul said.

The smoke from the valley blew down into their valley. The fire up there must have been pretty big because there was a lot of smoke.

Soon they heard sirens and it sounded like the fire department was on the way. They were up on the town road in the upper part of the hill.

A few minutes later a helicopter came over and it started circling the valley. It came over the house and hovered. Paul waved to it and pointed to the three drug guys on the ground. The pilot waved back and moved back up to the valley.

Ten minutes later they saw dust rolling up the driveway into the farm. The first two cars were from the Sheriff's department and the third was their parents. The Sheriff's deputies slammed to a halt throwing up a cloud of dust. Four deputies jumped out with their guns drawn and ran to the guys on the ground.

Paul and Anton were still sitting in porch chairs with two pistols trained on them.

"You can put the guns away. Good work guys," one of the deputies said.

The boys put the guns on safe and laid them on the table. Their parents came running up onto the porch and grabbed them and hugged them.

"Are you okay?"

"We're fine. Anton has a hurt shoulder."

"Did one of these guys do that?" his dad asked.

"No the guy who did that is still up in the valley I think."

"Up in the valley? What were you guys doing up in the valley?"

Paul looked at Anton and rolled his eyes.

"Well, it's kind of long story."

Chapter 53

"I thought we told you guys to stay away from that place," their mom said.

"Well I couldn't just let Paul up there. I had to go and try to rescue him."

"Did you start the fire?"

"Well I might have. I took some fireworks up to cause a diversion so Paul and I could get away. They'd been cutting the pot and had a lot of it stacked in piles and I guess it might have been a little dry. I think one of the Roman Candles landed in a pile and set it on fire. Once that got going, the whole thing went up."

There was some talk on the radio. The deputy listened and then answered someone on the other end.

"They found one guy tied up. The others left him behind. I guess these three were looking out for themselves rather than save their pal."

"Real honor among crooks," Paul said.

"As far as the pot field goes, there isn't much left. The Fire Department got down in there and put out the fire but most of the pot was burned up."

"So they might not get arrested for pot growing?" Anton asked.

"Oh they'll get arrested. There was a shed up in the valley that had several bags of pot that was all ready to market. They found all of their growing tools and stuff too. They'll be going away for a while."

The deputies loaded the pot guys into their squad cars and drove off. The boys and their parents went into the house.

"Well as upset as I am that you took such a chance, I have to say it came out pretty well," their dad said. "We should take you and have that shoulder checked out," he said to Anton.

"It feels a lot better now. Let's wait until morning. If it's still hurting we can do it then."

"We're sorry for getting into trouble but it all kind of happened so fast we were in a mess before we had time to think about it," Paul said.

"We need to have some dinner and a long rest and then tomorrow we'll start cleaning up and fixing the storm damage."

Anton's shoulder was much better the next morning. There was a bruise on the top of his shoulder bone but he was able to use it so they just let it go. They took a look at what they needed and drove to town and picked up siding and shingles to fix the house. They also bought a new tent for up at the pond. The old one was pretty well worthless.

They spent the next two days fixing up the house and then the boys went up and got rid of the old tent and put up the new one.

"You know we should dig open the entrance to the cave too," Anton said.

"Yeah, I suppose so."

They got the chainsaw and spent two days cutting the tree that fell on the entrance up into firewood and then digging all of the dirt and rocks from the entrance so they could get into the cave again.

That night they decided to fish until dark and then sleep in the tent. The dogs ran and played while they fished and then they built a campfire and sat watching the flames.

"Well what are we going to do now that those bad guys are

gone?"

"I don't know," Paul said.

"It'll be kind of boring around here without a drug cartel operating up there."

Paul laughed.

"Well I think I can live without them."

They crawled into their sleeping bags and Paul turned out the light. Patrick snuggled down by Anton and Sandy lay down next to Paul.

"What do you think the odds were for a second tornado to come up this valley?" Anton said.

"It has to be gazillion to one."

"Yeah, I suppose so. I'm sure glad we made it to the cave."

"Me too. After what happened to you, I sure wouldn't want to take a ride on one of them."

"The boy who fell from the sky."

"You must be one in a million," Paul said.

Anton nodded.

"When it happened I actually wished I'd have died too. My mom and dad were gone and I'd lost Patrick."

"But you didn't and now you have a new life Anton.

"Yeah, I know. If I hadn't lost everyone I loved it might have been pretty cool to survive a tornado."

"You have new people who love you."

"Yeah, that's for sure."

He reached over and squeezed Paul's shoulder.

"Goodnight."

Chapter 54

The authorities never caught the rest of the dope growers but they destroyed the camp. The owners of the property were being sought but there were so many dummy companies in the line leading to the real owners they might never get to the top.

Anton's shoulder was still sore so Nancy took him to the doctor and he got an X-ray. It showed a tear in his shoulder cartilage. He gave Anton a sling to wear for a week and thought it would take care of the problem

"That sling kind of puts me out of commission," Anton griped.

"No bike riding, no swimming, no fishing," Paul said.

"That sucks," Anton said.

"Oh well, listen I'm going to drive into town and get some propane for the camp light. Want to come along?"

"I think I'll just wait here. I want to look at some more drones that might do better stuff."

"Okay, I'll be back in an hour or so."

Anton watched his brother drive off. He sure hit it lucky to get him for a brother. There hadn't had one cross word between them in all the time they'd been together.

He got out his laptop and started scrolling through drones. His shoulder was aching so he took a pain pill that the doc had given him and laid on his bed with the computer.

The dogs jumped up on the bed next to him and curled up for a nap. He petted each of them and then lay back on the pillow. He was drowsy from the pain pill.

Anton woke when he heard the dogs barking. He looked around and blinked, trying to get focused.

The dogs were in the living room barking like crazy. He got up and walked through the house to the living room. There was a man at the door.

"Patrick, Sandy, no!"

The dogs looked at him and stopped barking.

"Hello," the man said.

"Hi, what do you want?"

"Can you put the dogs somewhere? I am not comfortable with dogs."

"What do you want?"

"I need to talk to you about the drug people."

"You know about them?

"Yes, I have information."

Anton called the dogs into his bedroom and shut the door. When he got back to the living room the man was standing in the house.

"Are you the young man who destroyed the pot crop?"

"Yeah, who told you to come in?"

The man pulled a pistol from his back pocket.

"I do not need an invitation."

Anton looked around trying to think of a way out.

"Don't try to run. I have associates outside. If you run I'll kill the dogs and burn the house down."

"What do you want with me?"

"I want to make an example of you. So other nosey neighbors like you will get the message to keep their noses in their own business."

He yelled something in Spanish and another guy came into the room. It was one of the guys from the pot farm that must have gotten away.

"He is the one. He has a big mouth for such a small boy."

"Tie him up."

Anton's right arm was in a sling because of his shoulder so the guy tied his left hand behind his back and wrapped the rope around his chest. The two guys led Anton outside. He looked around and there were no vehicles.

"Take him to the grow site," the boss said.

The guy who tied him up jerked hard on the rope and started leading him up the valley toward where the pot field used to be.

"I can only hope that Paul gets back," he thought. He'd read of what drug cartels did to their enemies and it terrified him.

Inside the house Patrick and Sandy were standing up looking out the bedroom window. They saw Anton being led up the valley. Patrick began howling wildly and Sandy pawed at the window trying to get through it. They were frantic.

When they got to the fence Anton saw a hole that had been cut through it. It was pretty obvious that they weren't coming back here after today. But did they come back here just to settle the score with him? That didn't make a lot of sense.

Back at the house, the dogs clawed at the door and had wood chips strewn all over the room. They both were clawing at it and barking.

Paul drove up and parked. He got the two cans of gas from the back and started for the garage. He could hear the dogs going nuts in the house, so he sat the cans down and walked to the porch.

"Anton, what's wrong with Patrick and Sandy? Anton, where are you?"

He looked around and the house was empty. But he could hear the dogs in their bedroom so he walked back and opened the door.

Patrick and Sandy nearly ran him down. They galloped out

to the living room and stood at the front door barking. Paul looked at the mess in the bedroom and got a feeling that something was very wrong.

He went out to the living room.

"Dang, the dogs are going crazy. What the heck happened here?"

The dogs stood with their paws on the door barking. He opened the door and they took off up the valley.

"Oh man, this looks bad," he thought.

He pulled out his phone and called his dad and told him what he'd found at home.

"I'll call the Sheriff. Get the dogs back and wait for me to get there. Do not go up to that pot farm," his dad said.

Paul clicked his phone off. He hesitated and then he went to the gun rack and took down a 12-gauge shotgun. He opened the drawer on a cabinet and put five shells into the gun and another five into his pocket.

"Sorry Dad, I can't wait for the Sheriff."

Chapter 55

Paul drove the Mule up to the pond. The dogs were at the fence trying to find a way though. He made them get back and he crawled under the fence. He dragged a log over to the fence and blocked the hole he'd crawled through.

"You guys have got to stay here. I don't want you getting shot."

He started up the valley and the dogs stood whining on the other side of the fence.

Anton's shoulder was hurting very badly. The pot dealers had him tied so tightly that his shoulder was being wrenched the wrong way. The boss of the guys that had been there before the place went up in flames was dragging him along through the woods.

"Hurry with that kid. We must dig up the cash and then we'll show these people what we do to those who interfere with our enterprise," the new big boss said.

They finally got to the old camp. Everything was pretty much destroyed. The shed was nothing but a pile of burnt boards and some blackened cans and equipment.

The guy tied Anton to a tree. He was exhausted so he slid down the tree and sat on the ground. His shoulder was hurting very badly.

"The Sheriff he was not so smart. He did not see our little safe," the big boss said.

"Clear it out here. Hurry we must get the money and get out of here."

The two other guys kicked debris off to the sides and then took a shovel and dug into the dirt. The shovel hit something metallic right away. They scraped dirt away and soon they had an area about four-feet square cleared off.

"See little smart boy, you were not so smart to find our cash."

Anton had no idea why they thought he was after their cash. All he wanted was to be left alone, but they'd messed with him and his dogs and he wasn't going to stand for that.

One of the guys got an iron bar and they slid it under the edge of the steel plate and pried it up. They got their hands under the edge and slowly lifted until they could tip the thing over onto the ground.

It landed and stirred up a huge cloud of dust and ashes that flew into the air. When the dust cleared a bit, Anton could see what they'd been digging for. There was a metal box buried in the ground that was about three feet square. He couldn't tell how deep it was but he knew one thing. It was full of plastic bags of money.

"Get it out!" the new boss said.

One of the guys knelt down and began handing bags of cash up out of the hole. Then he got down in the hole and Anton could see it was about three feet deep too.

"You see boy, we lost our product but he have our cash. There is over one million US dollars here. Not so bad hey?"

"Listen mister, I wasn't after your money. All I wanted was to be left alone but your cowboys here shot a dog and then threatened me, and my brother. That's why we crossed your fence."

"Well you cost us a lot of money in time and product. When the authorities find you the people around here will see that it is best to keep your nose out of others business."

The money was all out of the hole and the two guys stuffed the bags into four large canvass bags. They started to carry them up to the highway.

"Now little man, time for you to go in the hole."

Anton knew he couldn't get away. All he could hope for was to be able to lift the steel off once the pot guys were gone.

The first two came back and one untied Anton and roughly tossed him into the hole. The two of them strained to lift the slab of steel and they dropped it on top of the steel box with a loud clang.

Inside it was pitch black. Anton felt the walls. They were all smooth. He knew he couldn't lift the slab. His breathing was very fast.

"Please God, help me."

Chapter 56

P aul got to the old camp just as two of the guys lifted canvass bags up onto their backs. The other was dressed like a businessman and seemed to be the boss. They didn't see him as he snuck up from below them in the valley. He looked all around and couldn't see Anton.

He had two choices. Let them leave and hope he could find Anton or stop them and make them tell him where he was.

The three guys stopped in their tracks when Paul shot a load of 00 Buckshot into the tree over their heads. The old boss guy reached for a gun on his hip and Paul fired another shot right next to him that took a big chunk out of a tree.

"The next one will be dead center in the middle of your back pal. Throw that gun over in the grass."

The guy carefully tossed his gun into the grass. The other old guy from before also tossed a gun.

The new guy turned and smiled at him.

"Son, you have no reason to be threatening us with a gun. This is my property. We have a right to be here. We are not hurting anyone."

"Where's my brother?"

"I do not know your brother."

"Listen mister, I came home and my brother is missing. The dogs led me to your land. I have reason to believe you have him and I want him back right now or I'm going to start shooting holes in people."

The guy looked at the other two and made a motion with his head. The old boss started to move to the side.

"One more step and I'll blow your damn leg off. I don't know if you folks know what 00 Buckshot will do but I guarantee you'll be impressed."

The new guy smiled and stepped toward Paul.

"I'm sure we can work things out. Those bags contain cash, lots of cash, we would be happy to make a deal with you."

The guy stepped another step closer. Paul glanced at the other two with the bags and out of the corner of his eye he saw the new guy reach behind him. Paul stepped forward and just as he did the guy's hand came from behind him with a pistol in it. Paul brought up the butt of his shotgun and hit him in the forehead. He went down like a bag of cement.

"Anyone else?" Paul asked of the other two.

They both shook their heads.

"Where's Anton?"

The one that was just a worker looked toward the slab of steel on the ground.

"Lift that up," he said to the two of them.

They walked to the steel and grunted and groaned and lifted. Anton blinked up into the bright light.

"Paul holy crap... I'm glad to see you!"

Paul helped Anton up out of the hole.

"Are you hurt?"

"My shoulder hurts but I'll be okay. They had that hole full of money. The rest is up at the road."

"I called Dad. He told me not to come up here and wait for the Sheriff."

Anton grinned.

"You'd think he'd get used to the idea that we don't listen very well, wouldn't you?"

Paul gave Anton the shotgun.

"Can you shoot it with your shoulder like it is?"

"I don't have to aim. I'll just shoot at the middle of them if they move. Maybe a little lower than the middle. Maybe I'll make them an IT."

Paul tied the two guys up and then tied the boss who was out cold. They sat down to wait for the Sheriff.

They weren't sitting very long and they heard something in the brush and here came Patrick and Sandy on the run.

"I told them to wait," Paul said.

"They listen like we do," Anton said laughing and petting the dogs.

Chapter 57

The Sheriff arrived a few minutes later. A car came from the north and another from the south and they boxed in the van the drug guys had parked at the driveway to the valley. They came down the road with guns drawn and were surprised to see all of the bad guys tied up.

"You two have been busy," one deputy said.

"Well things kind of happened fast and we had to make it up as we went," Paul said.

"Well, you did a good job."

They called on the radio and soon more deputies showed up. They hauled the three drug guys up the road. One stayed behind to get the boy's statements. While they were doing that, their dad came walking down the road.

He looked at Paul.

"Didn't I say to stay out of here?"

"Dad, they had Anton, I couldn't just sit home and let something happen to him!"

"So everyone is safe?"

"Everyone is safe and the drug guys are in custody and their stash of money has been confiscated."

"What stash of money?"

"That's why they came back here. They had a pile of money buried over there," Anton said pointing to the hole. "They threw me in the hole and were going to leave me there. If Paul hadn't come, I might be suffocated by now."

"Well, then I guess that changes things," their dad said.

When all was said and done, it turned out that the big boss was on the FBI most wanted list. He was one of the biggest drug dealers in Mexico. With all of the evidence the boys had provided, he was tried and found guilty and sent to prison.

The farm where they'd been growing the pot was off limits until the trial was over because it was part of a crime scene. Afterward they found out it would be sold at auction by the government.

"I wish we could buy that," Anton said. "We could open up my old trails and jumps. We'd have a mega-bike course."

"Maybe whoever buys it will let us use the woods," Paul said.

Summer was almost over and the boys started school. They had a hard time leaving Patrick and Sandy home, but eventually they got used to it. Paul went out for football so Anton went to practice every day and then they rode home together.

Anton was waiting in the car for Paul to get out of the locker room when he saw a big black SUV drive up to the school office. Two guys wearing dark suits got out and went inside. A few minutes later they walked out and looked around. One of them pointed to Paul's car and they started walking toward it.

"Oh crap, what did I do now?" Anton asked himself.

The guys were almost to the car when Paul came out of the locker room. One of the guys stopped him and Anton saw him nodding and he pointed to him.

"That rat. He pointed me out."

Paul motioned for him to come over by him and the men. He got out and walked over.

"Anton these men are from the Government. They want to talk to you."

"I didn't do it. I didn't do anything."

The guys laughed.

"I'm afraid you did son," one said.

He reached into his jacket inside pocket and pulled out an envelope and handed it to Anton.

"That drug guy, the one that was the boss? You two boys helped us capture one of our top 10 Most Wanted. We've been after this guy for years. There was a reward, and now that he's in prison, we were sent to give you the reward."

Anton looked at the envelope.

"Open it," Paul said.

Anton ripped the envelope open. He looked at a check with a lot of zeros.

"Holy smokes it's for ten thousand dollars," he said handing it to Paul.

Paul looked at the check.

"It's not for ten thousand, it's for a hundred thousand. You missed a zero."

"A hundred thousand dollars? Are you kidding me?"

The FBI guys smiled.

"We confiscated several million in pot and cash. Once we sell the property and all of the vehicles this will be small change."

"When are you selling the property?"

"We're accepting sealed bids for it. The bidding will close in about a week."

"How much would it take to buy it?"

The two guys looked at each other.

"Well, we're not suppose to say but we've only had one bid. The problem with the land is that there's not much area to grow stuff and it's pretty remote. I'd guess sixty or seventy thousand would get it."

Anton looked at Paul.

"How do you put in a bid?"

Two weeks later the boys asked their parents to come with

them to town. They had something to show them at the county courthouse. Try as they might the parents couldn't get them to give them a clue as to what they were going to see.

When they got there they went to the Register of Deeds office. Anton and Paul told them who they were and the lady brought some papers out. They handed them to their dad.

"What's this?"

"It's the deed to the upper farm. Anton and I bought it. But you are going to sign the deed so it will be yours."

The parents stood there dumbfounded.

"You guys bought it? How the heck did you do that?"

The boys explained about the reward.

"So we bid seventy five thousand and got it. We're going to use the rest for another trail bike and some material for our bike cross-country course. We're going to take all the fences down and then we can use it for lots of stuff."

"A cross-country course?" their mom asked.

"Don't worry, we'll drive slow."

Anton and Paul worked all winter cutting brush and trees and building bridges across ditches and jumps. They took the dogs with them to the woods and the four of them had a wonderful time.

The boys became as close as if they'd been brothers all their lives. Anton often lay awake just before he drifted off to sleep and thought of his old family and Old Patrick but he wasn't sad anymore. He knew his parents would be happy that he'd had a chance at a second life.

"I've come a long way since that day when I fell out of the sky," he thought to himself. He looked down at Patrick sleeping on his bed. "All I needed was this guy," he said. He rubbed Patrick's soft ears and closed his eyes and went to sleep.

ABOUT THE AUTHOR

Dan Bomkamp has made his home in the Wisconsin River valley all his life with the exception of his college years in La Crosse. He has been an avid hunter and fisherman his whole life. For many years he was in the sporting goods industry and began writing in the 80s for outdoor magazines. He is active in the Foreign Exchange Student program having hosted 33 boys from 13 countries over the years. Golden Retrievers have also been a big part of his life. He had at least one Golden sharing his home for 33 years. He lives in Muscoda with his cat, Tigger and his Boston Terrier, Buster.

E-mail: Danbomkamp@live.com
Website: www.Danbomkamp.com

Other books by Dan Bomkamp

The Adventures of Thunderfoot
More Adventures of Thunderfoot
Thanks Thunderfoot
The Gosey
Big Edna
Voyageur
Lost Flight
Tag
Whiteout
Spirit
The Lost Treasure of Bogus Bluff
November Gales
Bringing Ethan Home

Non-Fiction
River of Mystery

www.ingramcontent.com/pod-product-compliance
Lightning Source LLC
Chambersburg PA
CBHW071155260626
47162CB00003B/1062